KAT DRUMMOND BOOK FOUR

NECROLORD

NICHOLAS WOODE-SMITH

Copyright © 2019

Kat Drummond

All rights reserved

This is a work of fiction. Any similarity to real persons,
living or dead, is coincidental and not intended by the
author.

ISBN: 9781704331768

Contents

Chapter 1. Evil

Those who try to understand evil can't help but become a little evil themselves. And those who slay monsters risk becoming the very monsters they have slain.

I tried not to understand evil. In my days fighting monsters and the human-monsters who brought them into the world, I concerned myself with only their deaths. The cessation of evil. But like any war, the fight against evil can only be won if you come to understand it. But by then, you have already lost.

It was a Saturday night and I had an essay on distinguishing vampire species due on Monday. Instead of working, I was hanging out with my friends, in a dark room, dimly lit by a television screening the Coen brother's *No Country for Old Men*. Its famous lack of music provided an eerie ambience, unfortunately overwhelmed by the sound of slurping, lips smacking and the exchange of saliva.

"Can't they find a room?" Treth, the appropriately prudish spectral knight living inside my head, whined. "I'm trying to watch the film."

I couldn't agree more. I'd brought myself as close to the screen as I could without hurting my eyes. This meant I was sitting on the carpet, holding my knees, a merciful distance away from my best friend, Trudie, and my (kinda) ex, snogging on the couch.

I concurred with Treth. I wished they'd find a room. I didn't know who instigated the impromptu make-out session, but all I knew was that it pushed me from the couch to the floor, where I was still struggling to watch the film that I'd been enjoying – until the inappropriate scene to my right drew my undue attention.

"What's even happening, anymore? Is the good guy dead yet? He was shot, right?" Treth asked, some desperation in his voice. He, like me, had been enjoying the film.

I rolled my eyes. I couldn't respond to him and was just as lost as he was. It was kind of hard paying attention under the circumstances.

Completely lost, I gave up on the movie and stood up.

"Kat?" Trudie asked, bringing her mouth away from Andy's just long enough to make my exit awkward.

"Going to check up on the others," I grunted.

She didn't acknowledge me. She'd returned to her debauchery, leaving me feeling disgusted and just a little bit jealous.

"I was enjoying it," Treth whined again, as I entered the hall.

"We'll watch it some other time," I whispered, just before entering Trudie's kitchen, where my friend, Pranish, and more-than-friend, Colin, were hunched over a laptop, some legal textbooks and a myriad of scrolls adorned with lawmancy script.

"Movie done?" Colin asked, looking up. Pranish continued typing away, the white-blue glare of the screen lighting up his face.

"No," I said. "Became a bit too crowded in there."

It was subtle, but I saw Pranish flinch, just a bit. He still didn't acknowledge me. He didn't need to. I knew he was absorbed with his work. I also knew that he really liked Trudie but considered himself too deep in the friend-zone to do anything about it.

"That's a shame," Colin said, scowling jokingly just a bit. "It's a great film."

"Great enough to re-watch it? It may not be too crowded in there if I had back-up."

Colin made a move towards the door, accepting my invitation, when Pranish spoke.

"Sorry, Kat. I need your boyfriend for a little longer."

I almost reddened at the title. He wasn't my boyfriend. We just hung out a lot. Neither of us verbally denied Pranish's assessment, however. I wondered what that meant.

"What are you guys even doing?" I sidled around the island-counter. The screen was filled with similar script to that on the scrolls but formatted like code. There were brackets around some of the magical runes and other mathematical symbols marring the already garbled text.

"The same thing I've been doing for months," Pranish muttered, still typing away. Colin gave me a faint smile and then looked back at the screen and a more readable legal textbook.

"This section," Pranish pointed at the screen. Colin leaned in and straightened his glasses. I loved it when he did that. Then I kicked myself for loving it when he did that. And then kicked myself for kicking myself.

My feelings are a bit complicated.

"Hmmm…there could be a loophole there if people sign using a proxy," Colin said, still reading.

"Suggestions?" Pranish asked, looking up at him.

"Besides preventing proxies? Let me check…"

Colin paged through one of the textbooks, rapidly. Pranish contemplated the screen.

I took a closer look at the screen and confirmed my suspicions. No English. Just lawmantic script. I only knew it was lawmantic script because of how often I'd seen it around Pranish and Colin. They'd been working together on this little project for a while now.

I smiled, faintly. Colin had been my attorney at a murder trial and now we were dating. More than that, he had been firmly entrenched into my friend group. Even my monster hunter buddies liked him. It was hard not to. Colin was a likable guy. He was diplomatic, empathetic, incredibly helpful and very smart.

And I couldn't help but think he was very cute.

"I didn't know you were a lawmancer," I said, impressed.

"I'm not," he responded, still paging through the textbook, and stopping at his destination. "I just know how to read it. I haven't been able to figure out the weyline channelling part yet."

"Lawmancy is a human spell-language," Pranish said. "Much easier for non-wizards to understand than the elvish and primordial stuff we usually have to memorise."

"It's like memorising case law. And it helps understand post-Cataclysm rulings. Can't do contract law these days without it."

His eyes scanned the page, and then he pointed at the screen and showed Pranish the page.

"A Lawmancer-Adept named Hanz Zechmann pioneered a stipulation that allows a proxy to have their obligations channelled to the true recipient."

"Does it require their true name? We can't expect people to give up their true names."

I frowned. I knew the danger of people knowing true names all too well. My childhood priest, the only person besides my now dead parents who knew my true name, had used it to sic some otherworldly demonic assassins on me. I'd survived but didn't want a repeat of the endeavour.

"This is the cool part," Colin said, excitement rising in his voice. I liked his passion for his discipline. "It only requires an essence of intent that can detect the consent of the true recipient."

"That's pretty dang cool," Pranish beamed. It was a rare sight these days. Pranish had helped me save Trudie from a bunch of vampires a few months ago and become traumatised during the experience. He was seldom happy any more. All that had saved him was his project. And I gotta say, it was a hell of a project. I didn't understand most of it, magic isn't my area of expertise, but I knew that it was revolutionary.

Usually, magic was the domain of old grimoires, tomes, scrolls and ancient tablets. The components used to transcribe the spell were just as important as the spell-words themselves, after all. Computers, despite being a technological marvel, were not considered sufficiently magical to contain spell-words. Printed paper couldn't even be used to produce scrolls without diamond or silver infused ink and special parchment.

This left spell production to factories of mages, who spent 12-hour days churning out magical texts to be channelled by wizards from around the world. It was labour intensive, costly, and made sorcerers even more arrogant, for their magic didn't require spells.

Pranish was a sorcerer, albeit a weak one. But he was not concerned with his spark and measly cryomancy. My friend was concerned with invention. With new ideas that could change the world. Combining his knowledge of IT with his knowledge of wizardry, Pranish had been spending the last few months developing a way of transcribing magical text onto a computer. It had been a gruelling few months, with no real progress, until I introduced Colin to Pranish. The two hit it off like dwarves and miners and had been working together ever since.

For, while the traditional spells of wizardry, originating from out of our world, could not be digitised, Colin and Pranish had discovered that a very human brand of magic could be combined with our technology: lawmancy.

The two were now working day and night to create a working build of magical software that could make traditional contracts irrelevant. It could make courts irrelevant!

As someone who had stood in the soulless grey halls of a courtroom before, I was very supportive of Pranish's project. I was not a big fan of the government, for a multitude of reasons. Colin and Pranish's project could circumvent a lot of the need for a public judiciary, making a large part of government irrelevant.

It may not be my area of interest, but I sure liked it in theory.

"What's the ETA?" I asked, trying to decipher the title of a lawmancy text. I think it said something about statutes of limitations.

"Hard to say," Colin said, before Pranish could send some sharp sarcasm my way. I liked Pranish, but he was very grumpy these days. Colin was not only helping him with the law and lawmancy part of his project, but also his PR. "Probably the beginning of November. Just before your exams."

"That soon?"

It was mid-September. A month since my run-in with an archdemon who had spared me after almost killing me. The archdemon had been serving Joshua Digby, my old family priest, who had sought to bring demons into the world and awaken a primordial titan to bring on the Rapture. The demon eventually revealed that he had never been Digby's servant and killed him.

In our final meeting, the demon warned me about more enemies in the shadows. People pulling Digby's strings. It was more to think about. Too much to think about. I was studying history, vampire lore and undead studies while holding down a job as a part-time monster hunter. Adding to that, there was a necromancer out there who had manipulated me in the past and then saved me from a horde of imps later.

It was all very overwhelming and that was if I didn't think about the mysterious purification magic I had unconsciously used once against a vampiric god and another time against the archdemon.

My life is complicated.

But at least I had some people in it who were not. While my feelings for Colin were complex, he was not. He was a good guy. And I knew I liked him. That extent of the like, and if it was an exclusive like, was the kicker.

Colin looked up from Pranish's screen as my phone rang, blaring the chorus of Fleetwood Mac's *The Chain*.

"Phone calls this late?" Colin asked, raising his eyebrow.

I checked the caller ID. Conrad. Of course, it would be Conrad. Either him or the private number of the tormenting necromancer.

"Your agent?" Colin asked.

I nodded and answered the phone, exiting the room so as not to disturb the two as they worked.

"Kat," Conrad said, his voice shivering with excitement and anxiety. It meant one of two things. Either a lot of money was up for grabs, or a lot of people had died. Conrad was hard to read. Many saw him as smarmy, but I had since learnt to appreciate the greasy man who helped me make so much money and kill so many monsters.

"Some time to be calling," I checked a silver wristwatch that Colin got me for my birthday, partly as a joke and partly because he's a sweetie. "1AM."

"Monsters don't sleep, Kat."

I sighed. I knew that very well.

"There's been an undead attack. A big one. A lot of people dead. A lot more people missing."

"Are the undead still there?"

"No."

"Not my problem then. There're countless undead in this city. I can't respond to every attack unless the perps are there to be slain."

"This is different. The attack stinks of our old friend, the Necrolord."

That had my attention. The Necrolord was a slang name for the necromancer who had come to dominate swathes of Hope City's underworld through mysterious mass acts of violence. I suspected that they were the same necromancer who had manipulated me months before and had saved me only last month when Digby left me to his imps.

"You are not meant to die. Not yet." The wight, an intelligent undead servant, had said to me.

Being helped by the undead had disturbed both Treth and me.

"Details?" I asked, my voice taking on an icy chill. That necromancer had a lot to answer for.

"I'll meet you at the site. A bar in Athlone on Jan Smuts Drive."

"Gotcha," I said, and was about to hang up when Conrad continued speaking.

"Kat, this is big," he sounded hesitant. A hint of worry. "Cops are all over the place. More than normal."

"No more doughnuts at this time of night to keep them busy."

"It's more than that. They asked for you by name."

I hung up and leant against the wall.

"They want us?" Treth asked.

I nodded.

"How do they even know about us?"

"I don't know. And that's what has me worried. Perhaps, Conrad has been running his mouth off?"

"That is his job, after all."

"Even then, I doubt it," I mused. "Conrad dislikes the Council as much as I do. He wouldn't blab to ticks, no matter how much money they were offering."

"Kat?" Colin asked, leaning around the corner.

I reddened. I hoped he hadn't seen me talking to myself. I could hear and sense Treth, but not even spirit-seers had been able to observe him. Only the archdemon had ever acknowledged him. I was glad about that. It confirmed that I wasn't completely insane.

"I've got a job," I said, avoiding eye-contact. I didn't want Colin to notice my apprehension. I had a lot to be apprehensive about. Colin may have seen me talking to myself, the cops asked about me by name and I was about to finally investigate the closest thing I had to a nemesis.

"This late?" Colin pulled a face. "Well, be safe."

"I will." I smiled, weakly. "Will text you when I'm done. Don't stay up too late."

I picked up my salamander hide coat off the hook, considered saying bye to Trudie, and eyed the glow of a laptop screen from the kitchen.

"Make sure he gets some sleep."

Colin nodded and disappeared back into the kitchen to continue his work.

I left without another word.

Chapter 2. Bar

My job had become a lot easier after I'd finally gotten my motorcycle license and used some of my savings to purchase a second-hand bike. I no longer needed to rely on taxis, buses or lifts from friends. It had gained me a freedom that allowed me to wage an even more efficient war against my monstrous prey. All it had taken was for me to finally go and apply for the license at the traffic department (horrific) and receive some intensive training from Guy Mgebe, a monster hunter who had ridden dirt-bikes since he was old enough to reach the handlebars.

The bar was easy to spot. White and navy-blue cop cars, their lights still blazing red and blue, were parked haphazardly across the road. A luminescent yellow tape was draped over the road, causing me to stop a walk away from the crime scene and make the rest of the way on foot.

It was chilly at this time of night, despite it being spring. I was glad for my salamander coat. It kept me appropriately warm.

Some cops, bearing polystyrene coffee cups, eyed me as I approached. I was quite the sight. Almost flaming orange coat, double-swords by my sides, and a metal face-mask covering the back of my head. I'd swivel it to cover my face if things got rough.

"This is a restricted…" one cop began but was touched on the shoulder by the other.

"She's the monster hunter. Let her through."

I eyed them up and down and ducked under the crime scene tape.

Conrad had been right. There were a lot of cops here. I'd never seen so many in one place. They were interviewing witnesses, cordoning off bloody tracks and guarding the ripped off doors of the bar. Conrad was leaning up against the wall next to the broken door. He saw me and waved.

"You were right," I said, eying the crowd of cops as they scurried around like ants. "Never seen this many ticks in one place before."

"They're riled like a dragon whose lost his hoard," Conrad replied, but his heart wasn't really in it. He seemed distracted.

"The Necrolord steal their doughnuts?"

"More than that," an unknown voice spoke up. A man in about his forties, with dark hair and a stern face appeared next to us, by the doorway. "The Necrolord has got us riled cause they've broken the law. As Hope City's finest, it is our job to respond."

If only they had responded when my parents were murdered. Hope City's finest were anything but fine in my books. I put more stock in bounty hunters.

"Kat," Conrad began. "Meet James Montague. He's an inspector with Hope City PD."

I offered my hand. I didn't like cops, but I'd be polite. James shook my hand, firmly. It was more than I expected. I imagined all Hope City cops to have limp wrists.

"Despite your disdain for my department," James said, his stern expression unchanging. "I'm glad that you are here. Your track record in dealing with the undead is unparalleled by any other single hunter."

"If you don't mind me asking, detective, why not Puretide? Individually, I may be the best, but Puretide has more resources."

"Puretide will be brought in on the case if necessary, Ms Drummond. In the meanwhile, we would like to work intensely with you. To get some of your insight into what we're dealing with."

He indicated for us to follow.

The bar was a mess. Tables were flung about, glasses and bottles smashed, and fresh blood stained the floors and furniture. I smelled rot. The undead had been here very recently. I also smelled another familiar scent. Gunfire.

"Was there a shootout, detective?"

"Some of the patrons of this establishment were carrying firearms."

He pointed to where some forensic cop types were depositing spent shells into plastic evidence bags.

"Anything short of a point-blank shotgun blast isn't going to do much to the undead," I added.

James eyed the hilts of my swords. "I gathered."

We made our way across the room, stepping over fallen chairs, glass debris and blood smears. I recognised some of the blood to be the black, pus-filled and gooey kind that spewed out of the undead. At least the victims had gotten some good shots off before they'd fallen. It was all some people could hope to accomplish. I got these jobs for a reason: most people can't deal with the undead the way I can.

"The proprietor, who has disappeared alongside his customers, had a CCTV system setup. The camera was hidden, which may explain why the footage is still intact," James continued.

Two cops were sitting at a laptop on the bar's dirty wooden countertop. At James' approach, they made way for us to look at the screen. I saw that the police laptop was connected to a computer underneath the counter.

"Play the footage, please," James said. The one cop, a cigarette in his mouth, clicked something to reset the recording and then pressed the space-bar.

The CCTV footage showed an 11:50 PM timestamp. It was colour footage, but grainy. I looked over my shoulder and saw a small speaker in the corner of the ceiling. If I squinted hard enough, I saw a blinking red light behind its mesh covering. The footage didn't show the outline of the mesh, however. It must have a one-way window enchantment, like my metal faceplate.

I turned back to the screen. The denizens of the bar were sitting at their respective tables, drinking quietly. It wasn't a club for young types like Trudie (I consider myself an old type). Everyone was keeping to themselves. Some were drinking alone. No shots. Just beer and fermented dairy. The footage went on and nobody commented. Conrad looked lazily at his phone and James stared intently at the screen.

Suddenly, chaos broke out on screen. Dust, splinters and debris obscured the footage. I saw people stand, suddenly, letting their chairs fall down behind them. A flash, and then another. Gunshots, probably. It was hard to tell. There was so much dust.

The dust cleared and revealed two dead men, icy shards in their chests, and a room of unconscious others. Pallid and stiff-moving undead, their skin flaky and bulbous, shuffled into the room. Their movements were jagged. Unnatural. As if they were being controlled by an invisible puppet master, manually moving their limbs one at a time.

"Flesh puppets," I said. Not many people knew the difference between different types of undead. "Corpses controlled directly by a necromancer. Like a puppet on strings."

"That one is missing a head," one of the cops pointed out.

"Flesh puppets don't need heads. The necromancer controls them limb by limb. Imagine them as literal puppets on necromantic strings."

I stopped speaking as another figure came into view on the footage. My heart skipped a beat as I recognised the undead man, moving much more fluidly and naturally than the rest.

He wore conquistador-style platemail, with a feathered wide-brimmed hat. By his side was a sheathed rapier. The tips of his fingers were icy, which explained the shards of ice sticking out of the gunmens' heads.

My recognition must have been noticeable, as James turned to me.

"You know that…thing?"

"It's a wight…I've run into it before."

"And it's not dead?"

"I was a bit restrained at the time."

"And you're not dead?"

"Let's just say that it was an odd situation."

"Odd, and suspicious…"

I hoped my glare pierced his soul. He looked away, fast, so it might have.

The flesh puppets were hoisting the occupants of the bar over their shoulders and carrying them out. The wight overlooked the work, and when they were out of view, looked at us through the camera.

"I thought you said that the camera was hidden," Conrad said.

"I thought it was," James replied. "I didn't watch this part."

He was visibly uncomfortable. His face almost white.

"He's toying with us," I said.

"He's a zombie," the one cop said, restraining a laugh.

"He's a wight." I'm sure I'd already said this. "He's sentient. Intelligent. Probably more intelligent than you."

"Hey…"

"How else do you explain how a group of undead that size could have attacked this joint an hour ago and still be on the loose?" I interrupted him.

"We have sent patrols across the area. Full APB."

"Then why does it seem like the entire PD is taking an extended fucking vacation outside?" I almost shouted.

Have I said that I really don't like cops?

There was a long, tense pause. Everyone in the room stared. I noticed a bead of sweat slide down Conrad's forehead, as he looked up from his phone. No one said a word. Had I gone too far? I usually kept my mouth shut for a reason. When I opened it, stuff like this usually happened.

The silence was broken by a slow and sarcastic clap. We turned, and I saw someone I never expected to see again in my life.

A man in his thirties, with pepper brown hair and a khaki trench-coat, entered from the burst open front doorway.

"Drake Callahan," James said. "You're late."

"I'm precisely on time," Drake replied, unfazed as he stepped over the debris in the room.

Drake was the private investigator who had been abducted by the Blood Cartel while investigating a mimic. The same mimic I later killed and the same Blood Cartel that I later dissolved. I had saved Drake's life, but he had also indirectly saved mine by warning me about the mimic through his self-written obituary.

"Ms Drummond," Drake nodded in respect. I returned the nod.

The police were still red after my outburst and my anger was only just cooling off. Perhaps I had overreacted, but I couldn't help it. These ticks were lazing away here pretending to play hero while innocent people were being abducted for necromantic experiments. It was happening now as it had happened before with my family. And it wasn't cops that had eventually saved me. It was Puretide. Private sector.

I clenched my fists.

"Calm down, Kat," Treth said. "This isn't helping."

Drake noticed my fists and laughed.

"Always fiery, aren't you, Ms Drummond?"

"Fiery is putting it mildly," James added, through gritted teeth.

"Kat," Drake said my first name, but I didn't mind. I liked the PI. His expression was serious, now. "James here is a friend. I trust him. And I know cops aren't our usual cup of tea, but James is one of the goodies. He'll do what it takes to get those people back."

I considered arguing, but bit back my retort. I nodded. I knew the people were as good as dead already. Cops didn't know how to deal with undead, much less wights as intelligent as this one. But if Drake vouched for James' sincerity, then that was (almost) good enough for me.

"So," Drake said, before there was an awkward demand for an apology. "Fill me in."

"Undead posse assaulted the bar at five to twelve. Was out in about 5 minutes. Witnesses outside claim they didn't see them. We're interrogating suspicious types now," James answered. He seemed calm again. Business as usual.

"We're dealing with a necromancer here," I added. "Cloaking magic, especially in a neighbourhood this dark, wouldn't be hard to pull off. Did the witnesses hear the gunshots?"

"Some did but say that gunshots are the norm in the area."

"How did the cops hear about it?" Conrad asked. I caught a glimpse of his phone's screen. Some colourful candy game. Looked too bright for my liking. I preferred grimdark.

"Patrol car phoned it in half an hour after the events transpired. They secured the area and witnesses while we issued an APB on the assailants. We've already phoned in the details of the creatures and the victims. If they can be found, they'll be found."

"A group like that?" The cigarette-smoking cop interjected. "We'll pick them up any minute."

"For your officers' sake, I hope not," I said, rolling my eyes.

The cop snorted. He disagreed.

"I'd take her words seriously, even if they're laden with snark," Drake said. "She's faced down more undead than any other individual agent in the city. Well, any agent that is still breathing."

"Her?" The cop snorted again.

"Enough," James said, pinching the bridge of his nose. "Ms Drummond, what else can you tell us?"

I considered glaring at the cigarette cop again but thought better of it. As much as I hated cops, I needed this case. I'd been wanting to be put on it for months. Finally, I was going to learn the truth behind my tormenter. The Necrolord was within reach.

I cleared my throat and continued. "Flesh puppets are not easy necromancy. They require a necromancer with precision and power. We're dealing with an extremely adept mage."

"That much is certain. What about the wight?"

"Wights are sentient undead. Usually, botched liches or resurrections. This particular wight referred to a *mistress* when it confronted me before."

"Mistress? The Necrolord is a woman?" James raised his eyebrow quizzically.

"That hard to believe?"

He eyed me up and down. "I guess not. Any other info?"

"The wight seems to be an accomplished cryomancer. A sorcerer in life, probably. What is unusual about that is that wights, especially magic using wights, tend to not have masters. Wights are considered botches because they slay their summoners more often than not."

"So, this is a loyal wight?"

"Seems like it. I am not privy to developments in the necromantic world, but assuming they haven't invented a compulsion spell, this wight must have been persuaded by its summoner to remain loyal."

"We know very little about the Necrolord," James said. "Only that they, or rather, she, has increased her control over vast swathes of territory in the slums. Entire blocks have disappeared, and other known necromancers have either disappeared or been found dead. Whoever she is: she is ruthless and powerful."

Drake was rubbing his chin, thoughtfully. James eyed him until he looked up and showed some shock at his surroundings.

"Drake, ideas?" James prompted.

"I was just wondering how they got out of here. Did the witnesses see any trucks, vans…etc?"

"None mentioned any, but we'll ask them again. Drummond, can flesh puppets or wights drive?"

"Possibly. But in the case of a flesh puppet, with a lot of difficulty."

"How do you know all this?" the non-smoking cop asked, some accusation in his voice. "I thought you just killed them."

"Undead studies. Getting some value out of my education," I answered, without looking his way. It was more than that, though. I had delved deeper into understanding necromancy. Know thy enemy, after all.

I stared at the now paused footage on the laptop. The graininess made it seem alive, but underneath it all was a faint shimmer.

I looked at my feet, squatted down, and stroked my finger across the floor.

Everyone, except for Conrad (who was playing his phone game), looked at me like I was mad. They may have even been right to think that. But a little bit of madness is good in this line of work.

I examined my finger. It was black with dirt, spilt liquor and grime. But also, something else…

"You feel it too?" Treth asked. I nodded to him, but made it seem like I had just come up with an idea.

"Months ago, when I was investigating the Eternity Lounge after the abductions, I felt dark magic in a part of the club. I feel it now. All over the floor, in fact."

The men looked uncomfortable. All except Conrad, who grinned faintly as he won a level of his game.

"It's harmless now – I think. But it also explains how the necromancer so easily abducts her victims. A miasma. Some sort of magical gas or wave, probably corruption magic, that renders its victims unconscious."

"What does this mean for us?" James asked.

"It means that we're dealing with a multi-disciplinary magic user. Necromancers often learn some corruption spells, but this miasma seems like high grade stuff."

"Very high grade," Drake interjected. "A miasma of this subtle power would require an expert corruption mage."

"So," James pinched the bridge of his nose again, closing his eyes. "We're dealing with an expert in necromancy and corruption."

"With a servant who is skilled in cryomancy," I added.

"This is bigger than we thought."

Of course, it is. You didn't think anything – I wanted to say.

"Okay, Drummond. Thank you for the help. We'll…"

His radio buzzed. He turned from the group and answered.

"Montague. Yes. Yes. Okay, sir."

He put the radio back on his belt and turned back to us.

"Drummond…" he said with barely hidden confusion and hesitance. "Would you, considering your track record against the undead, be willing to take a leading role in this case?"

"Leading role?" I asked, my eyebrow raised so high it threatened to merge with my fringe.

"It makes sense," Drake said, rubbing his chin again. "You've got an individual record that outstrips any Puretide agent. And, you have prior experience with the perp. At the very least, you will be needed as a consultant. With your hands-on skills, a leading role is a no-brainer."

I'm also a 20-year-old student with an assignment due on Monday, but I didn't tell them that.

"Kat will need the lion's share of the bounty plus the usual consultancy rate plus a mercenary pay," Conrad said, not looking up from his phone. This was new for him. Must be an addictive game.

"You can discuss that with my superiors," James said. He looked at me. "In the meanwhile, do you accept in principle?"

I didn't hesitate.

"If it means getting rid of this necromancer once and for all, then yes."

James offered his hand and we shook on it.

The night had grown colder as I walked back to my motorcycle. I sent Colin a text to tell him that everything was cool. Sure, we weren't a formal couple, but I'd check in with my other friends if they asked. The concern was sweet and made sense if you recalled my profession.

"It feels good," Treth said, a sense of triumph in his voice.

I looked around. The cops and some late-night onlookers were far away. Out of earshot.

"What does?"

"We're back on the crusade. The real hunt. Our real *raison d'etre.*"

Treth loved to pepper his speech with terms he picked up on Earth. Particularly, pretentious ones. Well, he learnt that from me.

"I agree," I said. "It's been too long. I find it odd that the ticks want me to lead the investigation, but if it means that I get to slice this monster's head off, then fine by me."

"You've gotten a lot less squeamish about killing humans," Treth noted, with a hint of concern in his voice.

"This woman, if it is a woman, has killed countless people. They aren't human anymore. They're monsters. And…"

"We slay monsters."

I nodded and arrived at my bike.

I don't know what it was, but something made me look up, towards the rooftop of the store opposite my parked bike. I stared, wordlessly, at the undead crow. Its single unrotten eye stared back.

"I'm coming for you," I whispered, and mounted my bike. I drove off, the crow's eye still on my back.

Chapter 3. Logistics

"Silver-plated?" the gunsmith asked.

I shrugged. "Sure. Might as well."

The old bespectacled gunsmith looked at the notes he'd been writing in ballpoint pen. He straightened his spectacles and stared at his notes.

"8mm? Are you sure. Very few guns use that calibre. 9mm will get more mileage."

I unholstered Voidshot, my magical C96 Mauser pistol, and placed it on the counter of the specialist gunsmith.

Timson Adleton had been a gunsmith before the Cataclysm, trying to compete with the mechanised military industrial complex. With the advent of enchanted weapons and munitions, he had found a new niche. Now, he crafted specialist ammunition for monster hunters. Brett had advised me to see him and, after having to barely slay a wraith with silverware, I felt I needed to upgrade my arsenal a bit.

Timson lifted up the pistol and examined it intently. It was connected to a silver chain on my belt, but there was enough reach for him to take a closer look.

"A fine piece," he said, and passed it back. "50 silver-plated 8mm rounds it is. Your license is on record, so shouldn't take too long. Do you mind waiting for about 15 minutes?"

"No trouble. Thanks."

I used my phone to wire my payment to Timson's account. He nodded appreciatively and disappeared into his workshop. I thought 15 minutes was ludicrously short, but wizardry had expedited the manufacturing process quite a lot. With a bit of metallurgy, good old automation and magical metal manipulation, Timson would have my bullets ready in a jiff.

I took a seat next to a display case containing a handheld repeater crossbow with a box magazine. I considered its inlaid crest – a stylised BH. I didn't know the logo. Timson didn't make crossbows, so I presumed the piece was just a collector's item used to show off his silver bolts, that glistened as the overhead light shone on them. I could see small seams in the blades of the silver bolts. They were designed to be a bit fragile. Upon impact with the werewolf or vampire, the metal needed to shatter, preventing the victim from pulling out the bolt and regenerating.

I'd only browsed last time I was here, while Timson added my license to his database. That took longer than the 15 minutes now needed to make the bullets. It seemed that not even magic could fix bureaucracy. I wouldn't even have this licence without Brett's help. He had done most of the administrative legwork for me. I had passed my competency test easily and just had to spend a day in the drab and grey Council offices in Old Town. Was all worth it to be allowed to carry Voidshot legally.

I really appreciated what Brett had done for me. I hated working with anything government-related. By doing most of the work, Brett had saved me hours of precious time away from overpaid civil servants. But it was more than that. I appreciated Brett the more and more I saw him. I first thought him annoying, but he'd proven himself capable. More than that, he had proven himself to be loyal, trustworthy. A good friend.

And, I'm embarrassed to admit, someone I might consider more than a friend.

But that was all very confusing. It didn't help that Treth didn't like him. Said he was bad for me and would end up hurting me. My mental room-mate kept pushing me towards Colin – which I didn't mind. Colin was cute and wonderful.

Did I just say that?

No, I thought it. But still embarrassing.

I reddened and decided to shift my thoughts to more pertinent matters.

"The Necrolord," I whispered.

"Yeah. Any idea how we're gonna start?" Treth replied.

I eyed Timson's workshop. The faint buzz of machinery and the hum of magic should drown out my whispering.

"For now, we need to wait for her to put her head above ground again. The slum is a quagmire. I don't know anything about it. The cops will need to find their leads there. Sounds like they've already started. Drake is putting together a dossier on gangs who have thrown their lot in with the Necrolord."

"Why would anyone serve someone like that?"

"Why does anyone do anything?" I asked, sighing and crossing my arms.

"You sound like the archdemon."

41

I snorted, and then answered. "He'd probably have some good insight on this situation. But I think we can muddle through ourselves. The gangs are doing what gangs do. They want wealth and impunity. They fear violence and power. The Necrolord can probably offer them wealth and relative indemnity, while scaring them with displays of power. I'd like to see a gang of hoods take on that wight."

I felt Treth's discomfort. "I wouldn't."

"Probably won't happen. By the sound of it, most of the slum-gangs have thrown their lot in with the undead already. That makes our job easier."

"I fail to see how."

"The Necrolord seems to value her secrecy. Otherwise, she wouldn't be nestling herself into the slums. If she values her secrecy, that means she has vulnerabilities that she needs to hide."

"And the gangs being on her side helps us in this regard, how?"

"Too many cooks spoil the broth. Too many people in an organisation, especially a secretive one, and someone will spill the beans eventually."

"So, we find one of the living accomplices to the Necrolord?"

I nodded.

"And then?"

"We find her stronghold. We raid it. I put down her army.

I hesitated, and then murmured.

"Then put her down."

"You really comfortable with that?"

"Does it matter? Those who beget monsters are monsters."

Treth nodded. We had a similar value system.

My phone rang. *Through the Fire and Flames* by *Dragonforce*. It had been playing when Brett picked Pranish and me up to slay vampires and save Trudie. It was now my ringtone for Brett. I answered.

"Hey Kats," he said. I could see his grin already. He found himself very funny. I liked that he was calling me Kats, like Trudie. I wasn't a fan of him calling me Katty. He still called me that sometimes, but it was becoming rarer. "What you up to?"

"Hey, Brett. At Timson. Getting ammo."

"Cool, cool," he sounded his usual carefree self, but there was a hint of hesitation and nerves in his voice. Very unlike him. He was usually so self-assured and cocky. Not the sort of behaviour you'd expect from someone who had been a child soldier in a death squad.

"So…the range got their overhead lights working again. That means that we can shoot at night," he finally said. Didn't sound like it merited the nerves. To me, at least.

"Cool," I replied. "If we can find the time. That's usually work hours."

"Was thinking we could do some shooting tonight. My treat. Got my shotgun back from lock-up if you're wanting to bruise your shoulder."

Sounded like fun, actually. I was used to bruises. But there was something…

"Oh, shit, Brett. That would be awesome any other night, but I've got a commitment."

There was a pause. "Sure, sure. Next time." He sounded chill, as usual, but there was an unmistakable hint of disappointment. I couldn't help but think – does Brett like me?

We spoke a bit about this and that afterwards and then we hung up. Timson arrived with the bullets and I left.

"What were we doing tonight, again?" Treth asked.

"Date with Colin."

"Another one?"

"I thought you liked him."

"I do, but not used to you doing…this."

"You rather we go shooting with Brett?"

"No!" Treth said, fervently. He disliked shooting and Brett. Preferred swords and Colin.

"Then the plan remains unchanged."

Yet, I fidgeted inside my jean pockets, not knowing if I'd made the right decision.

***

Colin treated me to a seafood paella at a nice relaxed restaurant at the Old Town harbour. I'd usually resist such charity, honour and all that, but he said he wanted to celebrate after winning a big case. Who was I to deny him buying me dinner?

We'd just watched the sequel to *Cry thy Pantheon*, starring Dionysus himself. Colin and I both had to refrain from laughing at the overacting Greek god. It was supposed to be a drama, but some things are better as comedies.

It was late and we were the last patrons at the restaurant. After we finished eating our meals (which were great, by the way), Colin drove me home.

Throughout the date, things went as normal. Colin was uncomplicated to hang out with. Easy-going. Could keep the conversation rolling. We discussed Pranish's mental health, the project, gossiped about Andy and Trudie, talked about some of his cases, about some of my jobs, and had a fierce friendly debate about *Star Wars* 16 vs 17. I finally conceded that 17 was slightly better, but only because it stopped wasting time on Jedi and focused on what viewers really wanted – more smugglers. I couldn't help but feel that debating Colin was a bit unfair, though. He was a lawyer. I was a monster hunter. We had different skillsets.

In the car, we continued to discuss the merits of particular sub-genres of sci-fi. It was cool to find someone else who appreciated spaceships when everyone else preferred dragons. There was still enough disagreement for a lively debate while Colin drove, however. He preferred space opera, while I was more a fan of cyberpunk. I liked the noire. The grittiness, and the anti-authority vibes. Colin preferred the exploration and wonder of space opera. Was fitting. He was the idealist, I was the borderline nihilist.

We passed the last set of traffic lights before my apartment and I was laughing at some half-arsed joke that was funnier if you were there. Colin was grinning, concentrating a bit on the road. Before I knew it, he stopped outside my apartment. I stopped laughing, and consciously lined up the traditional "thanks" and "see you sometime", but my lips didn't open. I didn't unbuckle my seatbelt. A heavy silence fell on the car, as I didn't act, and the previous casualness that I valued so much around Colin turned to awkwardness. But I could not blame him. I was the perpetrator.

I didn't know what was happening. There was a disconnect between my conscious and unconscious brain, and I was being taken on a ride.

It had been a customary evening. Colin was a great guy to hang out with. And while I called our time together dates, our relationship was still very much uncertain.

I couldn't help but feel that it was my fault. I was experienced in many things, but not dating. Not relationships in general. I just hadn't had enough time.

And with Treth in my head, it seemed somehow unfair. But with Colin, it felt different.

"Colin," I finally said, my voice quiet, uncertain. I avoided looking his way. His seatbelt was still on. Didn't hear the click. He must've been waiting for me. Waiting for what, I couldn't be sure.

"Do…do you…" I stuttered. What was I trying to say? How was I going to say it? Did I even want to say it? What if he didn't like what I said? Would it end all of this? End all these brief episodes of happiness?

But what if I didn't say the thing that I didn't know that I was about to say? Would Colin leave? Would I leave?

I didn't know. And the fact that I didn't know made me want to cry.

I opened my mouth to speak, but no words came out. I felt Colin's hand on mine.

"Let me walk you to your door."

I nodded and took a breath. I didn't realise until then that I'd not been breathing.

We unbuckled our seatbelts and left the car. The night air sent pangs of chill all over my bare skin. I wasn't wearing my salamander coat. Its glow in the movie theatre got me kicked out one time. Trudie then attacked the attendant and we got suspended from the Riverside cinema. Before I could shudder, however, I felt a warmth on my back. Colin had deposited his blazer over my shoulders. I looked at him and he smiled, warmly. I felt a pang I didn't understand.

We walked in silence to my door, where I stopped. And didn't move.

What do you want, Kat? I asked myself.

Do you like him?

I did. I really did. But did he like me?

Of course, he does, my rational brain said. *He wouldn't hang out with you like this otherwise.*

But my more dominant and angst-ridden brain said otherwise.

How could he like me? We were friends. Buds. He humoured the comments about our relationship being more than just friendship. We'd never discussed it ourselves.

We hung out because he found me fun. That didn't mean he liked me any more than as a friend.

How could he like me? I asked myself again. I was not feminine. I stunk of monster blood and necro-juice more often than not. I killed things for a living. I was a broken, shattered soul, who spoke to herself when she thought nobody was looking.

How could Colin, who was so great, like someone like me?

I almost jumped as I felt Colin's hand on my shoulder. I realised that I'd been standing in front of my door. Unmoving. I anxiously reached into my jeans pockets for my keys but stopped as he gently pulled me to face him.

I tried to avoid his eyes but caught a glimpse of his concern. If he saw into mine, what would he see? Would he see my dark blue eyes? Or would he see all the people I've killed? Would he seehow broken I was and all the horror I've had to face? Would he understand, or would he rightfully run away?

I felt warmth on my cheek. His hand was warm. Soft, yet reassuring. Would mine be as soft? They were covered in calluses and scars. Covered in blood and grime. From the dead and the living.

I looked into his brown bespectacled eyes, to see the horror that he must feel for one such as me. But I didn't see horror. I saw warmth, and something I didn't understand. I stopped breathing and my heart beat like a machine gun.

He leaned closer, and I could feel his breath provide some heat against the cold night air. I'd think human breath to always smell bad. Zombies used to be humans and their breath always smelled bad. But Colin's didn't smell like the rot of my prey.

I didn't know why, but I closed my eyes. It was something I seldom did, but it felt right to do it now. For the first time in a long time, I didn't feel that I needed to watch for danger. I felt a soft pressure first. On my lips, and on the back of my head and back as he held me. I was glad for it, as my legs became jelly.

The warmth on my lips grew and I forgot everything that I had been thinking. Every bit of insecurity. Every ill-thought and angst-ridden bit of self-loathing I had went into the In Between, to be nibbled on by demons and otherworlders. All that remained was me and Colin.

I opened my eyes as the warmth stopped. I felt a tingle by my lips, that were open just a little. I couldn't speak.

"Yes," Colin finally said, looking at me with a gaze I now understood. "I do like you."

Chapter 4. Abomination

Despite my date (which I now knew was a genuine date and not just a playful term for hanging out), I still managed to get my assignment in on time on Monday morning. I had Colin to thank for that. While I considered inviting him inside, much to my own shock, he bid me farewell and left. I was thankful for that. I know I'm twenty now, but I never really got an opportunity to develop like a normal girl. I didn't understand any of this, and now I knew that Colin knew this and he didn't care. He was fine letting me go at my own pace.

I still didn't know what to think. It was all confusing. But I knew that I had enjoyed it, and I really wanted to see Colin again. After he kissed me and left, I couldn't sleep, and spent all night finishing this assignment. In the morning, I wasn't even tired.

"And while vampiric blood transfusion doesn't cause infection, it does result in an addiction akin to more traditional narcotics," my friend and professor, Miriam LeBlanc, continued.

I wasn't taking notes. The butt of my pen was chewed to ribbons and I was staring fixedly at the top of the whiteboard.

How long until end of class?

Did it matter? Colin had work all day and tonight.

I considered sending him a text.

No, no. That wouldn't do. He was probably busy. I couldn't be too eager. Didn't want to chase him off.

But I wasn't going to chase him off. He liked me.

I couldn't help but grin stupidly. Miriam noticed and raised her eyebrow in my direction, before continuing.

"Recipients of vampire blood often exhibit temporary bouts of vampiric traits. Most often, regenerative capabilities and enhanced strength. Some even gain vampire weaknesses, such as an aversion to sunlight. But, do not be confused. They are still not vampires. They lack the anchor-point to the Dark World that makes a vampire a servant to their curse, and they cannot sustain themselves on blood alone. Rather, they are still human, but temporarily boosted by the proteins of a vampire's blood."

She eyed the class.

"And before you get any ideas, vampire blood isn't some casual drug you can just snort and leave after you're bored of it. It consumes its addicts. No vampire blood addict has ever been rehabilitated. This inevitably leads to the addict becoming a servant to a vampire – just to get their next fix."

That prompted a thought that did not concern Colin.

Was the Necrolord giving the gangs something that not only encouraged their servitude, but made the Necrolord invaluable to them?

Oh, shit. The Necrolord! I hadn't been thinking about my possible nemesis since before last night. I'd been consumed by Colin.

Bad, Kat, bad! I had a job to do. A crusade, as Treth would call it. I couldn't be wasting time with boys.

But…Colin.

My phone buzzed in my pocket. Fortunately, it was on silent. I surreptitiously checked the caller ID. It was James Montague.

He said he'd only phone in an emergency.

I looked at the whiteboard. I hadn't absorbed any info anyway, so might as well leave. Before the phone could stop ringing, I packed up my things and quietly left the lecture theatre. Miriam would understand. We'd first met when I had exorcised a ghost for her. She appreciated my job, even if it meant leaving her classes early.

"James," I acknowledged, once I exited the lecture theatre.

"Drummond." He refused to use my first name. "Big emergency. Get to Old Town. Gardens PD. Stat!"

"The Necrolord?"

"We don't know. It's a monster. Something undead. Something big. It's attacking the police station."

"Puretide?" I suggested, while I jogged to my motorcycle. It was parked nearby. This lecture theatre building was near the parking lot.

"They don't know what they're doing…"

I heard gunshots. Some pistols and shotguns. They wouldn't do much against most undead, never mind a monstrous-class undead.

"Get here, Drummond!" James shouted, and then hung up.

I rushed to my apartment on bike, running two traffic lights. I could get the PD to excuse the fines later. There were perks to working with the cops. I picked up my salamander coat, armour, face-mask, Voidshot and my swords and got back on my bike. Would be much easier if UCT wasn't such a naïve campus and let me carry my equipment. Would have meant a lot fewer dead people from the undead attack earlier this year. I didn't even stop to say hi to Duer as I rushed into my apartment to collect the weapons. Would need to apologise to him later. He was a little bit sensitive sometimes.

I revved my engines and took off.

"Kat?" Treth said, as I bobbed and weaved through traffic.

"What?" I shouted over the cacophony of traffic and rushing of wind. I accelerated hard as a truck tried to overtake me. I caught a glimpse of a very rude gesture from the driver.

"What happened last night?" Treth asked, almost sheepishly.

"Is this really the time?"

I almost got hit by a car as I took a sharp turn onto the freeway.

"You didn't answer me last night."

I didn't recall him asking. Was I really that out of it?

"I knew you liked him," Treth said, stopping as I almost pranged into the back of a bus. I dodged and kept down the middle of the freeway. "But, you were catatonic last night. I couldn't guess what was inside your head."

He obviously didn't know what was inside my head right now either – an intense desire to not be destroyed in traffic as I raced against time to save people from a monstrous undead.

"Can we leave this for another time?" I asked, through gritted teeth.

"Can it be…" Treth started, and I felt a mischievous grin cross his lips. "That was your first kiss?"

I almost ploughed into the back of a pick-up truck, only managing to skid onto the off-ramp and into Old Town. Guy's intensive training had really paid off.

My face was blistering red underneath my helmet.

Damn Treth! Was he trying to get us killed?

He mercifully stopped speaking, and I managed to get my bearings and ride much more adeptly towards the Gardens in Old Town.

The Gardens was a lusher area of the usually overwhelmingly urban Old Town of Hope City. A decent weyline had led to a previously mundane historical garden becoming a lush and verdant park. Nearby buildings had been converted into housing and restaurants, showing off modern and restored colonial architecture that led to a beautiful environment – if not for a single drab 70s-style concrete block that was home to one of Old Town's police stations.

Traffic was backed up leading into the Gardens district. So much so that I skidded my bike to a halt, hoped it was secure enough parked outside a fish and chips shop, and ran the rest of the way. Gunshots were my guide. Gunshots and screaming. As was often the case, bystanders stood at a distance, watching in the direction of the cacophony as if stealing a glimpse of a concert they hadn't paid for. I rushed past these onlookers, paying no heed as my coat singed a few along the way. My coat had a propensity to burn things when it felt it necessary. Apparently, now was the time to start burning things, including people's briefcases, a local election poster on a lamppost, and people's elbows. The flames never harmed me, but they made a mess of everything else.

Closer to the gunfire, I saw people running away. I stopped one of them, a sweaty woman wearing a blue and grey jogger's outfit. She looked at me like a unicorn in headlights as I held onto her arm.

"What is it?" I shouted over the traffic, sirens, gunshots and screaming.

"A monster!" she yelled and tried to wrest herself away from my grasp.

Monster? Very helpful.

"What does it look like?" I insisted.

She looked at me like I was insane.

"Like a bus made of dead bodies. Let me go!"

I did as she asked and let her renew her sprint down the street, towards the traffic jam of bystanders.

"A bus made of dead bodies?" I repeated.

"Sounds like an abomination," Treth replied.

I nodded. Abominations were undead created from at least ten corpses, moulded together to form disgusting monstrosities. Depending on the necromancer who put them together, they could be fierce opponents. I'd never fought one before, but Treth had.

"You know what this means?" I asked, renewing my run towards the police station.

"A necromancer. Very little chance it was rift-borne."

"Think it is the Necrolord?"

Treth hesitated, considering. He nodded. "Very likely."

I smelled the iron stench of blood and acridity of gunpowder in the air as I turned into the street adjacent to the Gardens. The police station was opposite the old St George's Cathedral, and the street in front of it was strewn with corpses and crashed, blood stained cars. The cops who weren't missing heads and limbs lay, barely breathing, as healers and paramedics tended to their less lethal wounds. I didn't see any monsters – dead or undead.

I drew my swords, more to comfort myself than because I immediately needed them and approached the surviving policemen. Closer to the scene, I observed the black blood of the undead stained on asphalt, sharp debris and crushed cars. The trail of destruction and black ooze led into the Gardens. I looked towards the Cathedral. Its old wooden doors were splintered, and a stained-glass window was shattered, its multi-coloured shards lying all over the floor.

"It went into the Gardens!" a paramedic confirmed, as I approached him, pale and wide-eyed. His hands were covered in red. His patient wasn't breathing anymore.

"What did it look like?"

"Could've been about eight metres tall. Maybe bigger. It was writhing underneath its flesh."

He shook his head, as if trying to will the image away.

"I need to know what this thing is if I'm going to kill it," I pressed.

"It looked like a giant mound of flesh, with hundreds of arms and legs sticking out. Had a huge mouth with a person for a tongue. The tongue…thing grabbed some of us. They could still be in there."

I didn't contradict him, but I knew better. Whatever was left of the people who were dragged into the abomination couldn't really be considered people anymore. They were either zombies, absorbed into the abomination, nutrients for the undead bodies, or even minions that could be dropped out.

I had read about abominations before. We'd studied them in undead studies. They were one of the more complicated types of undead. I once said that undead have patterns. That they're simple. In general, that's true. But every rule has exceptions. Abominations were the exception. They were more than an undead mutation. They were a totally new creature, stitched from an uncertain group of mutants. This formed an enemy that I couldn't really understand until I dissected it. But I'd need to kill it first, and that required understanding it. A nasty catch-22.

"Hunter," the paramedic continued, as he unconsciously applied compressions to the now dead civilian's chest. "There's a school on the other side. It's headed towards the school."

My eyes widened, and I found myself running towards the Gardens before I could register the information. I followed the trail, leaping over gore-stained debris and sliding over the fronts of crashed cars.

This creature had killed so many people. Had destroyed cars and structures by itself. Could I really handle it alone?

Gunshots rang out in the distance. Towards the school.

I didn't really have a choice.

The Gardens would have been peaceful if not for the gunshots in the distance, the trail of blood and corpses, and the pounding in my chest. The creature had broken through hedges and over trees, breaking branches and even knocking over smaller trees. At least it wasn't strong enough to knock down the fully grown ones.

"Puretide corpses," Treth observed.

I slowed down. He was right. Just ahead, where the trail of destruction continued, there were the pulverised and eviscerated corpses of white-clad men. Their rifles and pistols had been crushed during whatever skirmish had killed them. Just as well. They wouldn't help me. They sure hadn't helped their now dead owners.

I sped up again, my blades swinging by my sides, when I saw an unusual set of items on the chest of a headless corpse. A bandolier of dark green grenades.

I'm a simple girl. I see grenades, I take them.

They wouldn't do so well against the abomination if it could absorb as much flak as I suspected, but they could become useful.

I sheathed my swords and swung the bandolier over my shoulders. The grenades weighed me down more than I was comfortable, but I was still nimble enough that they wouldn't be too much of a burden. And, hey, who'd pass up on some free grenades?

As was usually the case with the undead, I smelled the creature before I saw it. Was like someone had set fire to a pile of rotting meat and assorted trash. I could smell the heat mingling with the usual sour scent of decay. Undead were normally cold, but magical energy did emit heat in high amounts. This abomination was probably a sauna on a hundred legs.

"Careful, Kat," Treth whispered, even though only I could hear him. "Slow and steady. Recon before fighting."

I gritted my teeth. The lives of children were at stake. But he was right. I needed to be careful. Couldn't save anyone if I was dead.

I slowed and moved towards a tree. With my back pressed to the bark, I peeked around the corner.

The creature was huge. I didn't know if 8 metres tall or more. The first woman's description was more accurate. It was like a bus made of dead bodies, but all blended into one pale pink, pulsating blob, with arms and legs bristling out of its flesh like hairs. Four large leg-like limbs held it up, as it considered a spiked wall. A lone policeman was still firing his pistol, as a Puretide agent dragged half his mate's body to the treeline. The abomination ignored the humans, as it probed the high wall. I heard the fire alarm going off in the buildings on the other side. Hopefully the kids would all get out in time.

The wall buckled as the abomination put its front legs on top of it. The cop's pistol emptied and he reached for a mag that wasn't there. The Puretide agent realised that his friend was dead and he collapsed onto the ground.

What was I supposed to do?

"Treth, how did you kill these things?"

"We had mages," he said, a hint of desperation in his voice. "Their hide is flimsy, but they can take a lot of damage. Swords and spears did nothing. Only fire and magic had some sort of effect."

"Where's a fucking sorcerer when you need one?"

My hand tensed on the hilt of my sword. I saw a crack form on the wall to the school. The cop, his pistol depleted, picked up a branch and charged.

Charged. A small man, against a giant beast. And he charged it.

He didn't survive long. But he made me spring into action. I sheathed my swords and drew Voidshot. I advanced on the creature, as it squashed the cop into a paste. The Puretide agent stared on in horror, cradling the corpse of his friend.

I fired. The magically enhanced bullet went wide as the writhing morass turned back to the wall. How could I miss such a big target?

I fired again. This time, I found my mark. It reared up like a speared elephant and turned on its heels towards me. While the conventional rounds from the cop weren't scraping it, Voidshot was designed to hurt the usually unhurtable. I wasn't convinced that my gun would be able to kill it, however. Wasn't counting on it.

The creature faced me and, with a roar, opened its maw to reveal a horde of screaming, lifeless people. They were coated in black and red blood, waving their arms and begging for help they could never get. They did not have the jagged movement of flesh puppets, or the hungry aggression of zombies. They looked like distressed humans. I had to remind myself that they were dead. I couldn't save them. I could only put an end to the charade.

A thick fleshy tendril extended from the maw, bearing a naked woman, her arms and head hanging limp.

I aimed again and fired. The shot hit the woman-tongue in the chest and she looked up with hollowed eyeholes. She screamed, spewing blood.

I turned and ran back the way I had come. The thud of flesh on gravel and concrete told me that the chase was on. I just hoped I could outrun this thing.

"Restrict its movements, Kat!" Treth shouted.

I caught a glimpse of the fleshy beast tearing its way towards me, spewing blood along the way. It knocked over trash cans, tore up benches and snapped branches along the way.

"Easier said than done," I replied, in between breaths. The grenades on my chest were making this sprint much harder than normal.

Treth was right. I needed to get it in a smaller environment. It was big. Big enough to crush cars. But if I could get it somewhere where its size would impede it, then I could find a vulnerability. I heard a tree snap and fall.

The question was: what could hold it?

"Between those trees!" Treth ordered.

I turned to where his spectral inclination pointed. Two large trees with trunks as thick as the creature itself.

I also caught a glimpse of the monster. It was gaining. I could practically feel its nauseating heat rolling off it. I was panting. I had pretty good stamina, but this was a bit too much even for me. I needed to slow it down.

I rushed between the tree-line and turned. It hesitated but roared after me again as I coaxed it with a bullet to the forehead. I stayed still, the trees flanking the opening before me. I hoped that it'd be enough.

The heat grew closer and the stench more overwhelming.

It squelched as it impacted with the sides of the trees. Black blood oozed out of invisible orifices and its bristling arms flailed.

I grinned. It was wedged between the tree trunks. Firmly. Its hair-like arms bristled with distress as it attempted to heave out of its entrapment.

"Didn't think this'd work."

As was my luck, however, I heard a creak. And then a crack. The trees rumbled, and their leaves started to fall in droves as the trunks shook. The beast continued to pull towards me, edging closer and closer, pulling the massive trees along with it. The tongue-woman screamed at me, staring with lifeless red-white eyes.

"Um, Kat…" Treth said, as I backed away slowly. "Time to start running again."

I did so. Fast. The pain in my chest from the exertion was easy to ignore with the lumbering creature gaining fast on my heels.

"So, wood is not good enough," Treth said, dully.

"I need to figure out a way to kill it, Treth!" I shouted and regretted it as it slowed me down just enough for the creature to knock me into the treeline with its long tongue.

I tumbled over the bushes, which broke my fall. I was gonna have a wicked bruise on my arm. If I survived this, and that was becoming increasingly doubtful.

"You okay?" Treth asked.

Do I look okay? I wanted to shout, just as the abomination loomed above me, the hollowed eyes of its victims staring at me despite their particular lack of eyes.

I rolled just in time as the abomination's leg-like thing plummeted down on the space where I'd been lying. I pulled myself to my feet and felt my everything ache.

There had to be a way to win this.

Or not. This wasn't a video game. There wasn't necessarily a way to win. I could die, without there being any other alternative.

But I refused to accept that.

The creature lashed out and I managed to jump just out of the way, stumbling towards the edge of a dried-out canal. It wasn't deep. Standing at the bottom, its lip would only just be above my head.

It's typically not a good idea to take the low-ground against an enemy, but I was out of options. I dropped down and ran down the canal. The abomination followed above me, lashing out and emanating it's sickening heat. Like a swamp mated with a furnace. I was keeping my distance, but only just. I was flagging. Until I saw a small footbridge. I dove under it, into a small concrete pipe that a child would find fun. I'm no child.

The creature collided into the bridge and it shook but didn't break. I backed away but didn't exit out the other side.

"Any ideas?" Treth asked, his voice shaky. He was meant to be the one who'd killed these things before!

I looked at the other end of the pipe, considering trying to escape, and then turned back in the direction of the creature. The naked woman was there, crawling in, scraping along the rough concrete.

I backed away. It lunged, and I kicked it in the face. That only made it angrier. She screamed. A primal and rage-filled raw, more than one of fear. I tried to draw my sword, but the pipe was too small. I couldn't draw it. The woman drew closer, hissing and gargling. Black bile spewed from her mouth.

How was I meant to kill this thing?

The answer was pressing into my chest.

I somehow managed to manoeuvre the bandolier off my shoulders, while kicking at the monster snapping at my heels. Lucky for me, I had thick boots.

I kicked the woman in the face and then reached for my boot's shoelaces. I untied them as best I could in the action and pulled until they were almost wrenched out of their sockets. The creature was still roaring. I heard some cracking and gut-wrenching squelching as it pummelled the top of the bridge with its confusing appendages.

My hands weren't shaking despite my fear and adrenaline. I dextrously looped the shoelace through the pins of the grenades until the lace was taut. I didn't pull too hard in my testing but tightened the connection until I was satisfied with the tension.

I took a deep breath.

Here goes nothing…

I shot out of the other side of the pipe, leaving the woman grasping at nothing. I pulled my wakizashi with my right-hand, the grenade bandolier held to my left.

The creature loomed above me, but it was stuck inside the bridge, with its tongue still looking for me. I clambered over the bridge and felt its sweltering unnatural heat wash over me. It was like all the swamps in the world hit me at once. Its arms continued to flail. It was covered in the things. All except for a naked spot on the top of its back.

I tightened my grip on my sword and the bandolier and ran towards the thing, jumping just as I reached the edge of the bridge. I landed on top of a sea of arms. I kept running. Too fast for them to react. I kept my sword down, cutting into the arms and causing them to recoil.

One grasped my ankle, but I severed it and continued running. I was tired. Flagging. Only my coat kept most of the hands away, as it burnt their fingertips. The air was baking me in its stench. But I had to make it.

I landed on the clearing and dug my sword into its naked flesh. It cried out as I dug a crevice in its back, large enough for my payload. I used the shoelace to pull all the pins at once, then I kicked off the creature and fell onto the ground, bruising my knees. I ran for it, towards a concrete bench, which I took cover behind.

The creature freed its tongue from the pipe and looked towards me.

It exploded.

Mounds of pink and black flesh shot out like shrapnel. Pieces of bone stuck into the back of the bench, trees and walls. Some fleshy debris hit my coat and was scorched.

The horror-show was over in seconds.

I stood, with just a slight bit of pain in my leg where I'd been hit earlier. I limped towards what remained of the monster in the canal. None of its remains looked at all human. Very few undead could survive that. I doubted even this could. It was debris. Nothing more.

At the bottom of the canal, however, there was something else.

A message, scrawled in black-red blood, somehow singed into the concrete.

"Time to play, Kitty Kat. Catch me if you can."

Chapter 5. War

The Council was passive. It was immovable. Even during the crises of the Zulu annexation of the eastern frontier and the encroachment of the ogre hordes in the north, the Council could be counted on to remain apathetic. It didn't matter to them. The extent of their effort was posting up the occasional public bounty on a monster. For everything else, the people of Hope City were expected to fend for themselves.

But this time, things were different.

The abomination, right on the doorstep of Hope City's historic parliament building near Gardens, and the necromancer who controlled it, had rankled the Council in a way I didn't think possible. They didn't do the usual half-hearted clean up and bounty reward. They were furious. Upon my defeat of the undead, the Council not only paid me a handsome reward, they mobilised everything they had to find the Necrolord. Cops, the army, Puretide and Drakenbane. The MonsterSlayer App was afire with featured bounties against the undead, and a desire for information on the Necrolord.

I had never seen the Council so worked up and, while I agreed with the notion that the Necrolord had to be brought to justice, the Council's sudden energy was puzzling.

Conrad said that the last time they were this antsy was when a group of assassins went after the then Chairman of the Council, Adam Dawi. That was 15 years ago. Since then, the Council had taken everything in its stride. Zombie attacks, vampire cartels, orc raids. Everything. If it didn't threaten to sink the city underneath the waves, then it wasn't worth the Council's focus.

But not now. Now, they wanted blood.

I knew I should also want blood. The abomination had killed so many people. Had almost killed me. And it had been targeted at me. The Necrolord had created the entire thing just to send me a taunting message. What a sicko…

I felt a true anger at that. I did, but my mind was on other things. More, or less pertinent? Up for debate.

While the Necrolord was still at large, my mind was elsewhere. Particularly on the fact that I hadn't spoken to Colin since we kissed.

I found myself reading over the dossier that Drake had sent about some Necrolord aligned gang a fifth time without absorbing anything. My free hand was resting idly on Alex's head while my other hand was on the laptop keyboard. I had finally invested in a laptop. My recent hunts were getting prosperous and I really needed one. It was an entry-level Uhurutech model. Nothing fancy. Just powerful enough to run a word processor and some games with low system requirements. Colin, Pranish, Trudie, Andy, his friend Oliver, and I were all playing an old sci-fi online game loosely based on my favourite book series, Warp Wars. It was called *Age of Aegis*. I played a dual plasma blade wielding bounty hunter in the game (hey, I like the style), with Colin running a techmancer control build, Pranish on engineering support, Trudie on an alien tank and Andy and Oliver specialising in sustained damage as troopers

It was all good fun and helped me unwind after a long day of hunting and studying. Was much less stressful than tangling with an abomination, at least.

I considered the icon for the game in my toolbar, just below the dossier document from Drake. I sighed. I hadn't played it in the last few days.

"You're distracted," Treth said, matter of factly.

"I am?" I asked sarcastically.

I looked out of the window. Duer was tending to his plants. It was the day after the abomination hunt. I was still achy but had gone through worse. It was a wonder how. Besides the archdemon, the abomination must be the most threatening monster I've ever faced. It was definitely the most powerful thing I've ever killed.

And I couldn't help but shake the feeling that the Necrolord hadn't intended it to kill me. It was designed to give me a fight, but the Necrolord was convinced I'd overcome it. That sent a chill down my spine. If this was just a taunt, then what could the Necrolord accomplish when she or it was really trying?

"The question is," Treth continued. "If you're thinking about our mysterious foe, or…"

I closed my laptop suddenly. Duer jumped and looked at me through the window. When he saw that there was nothing amiss, he glared and went back to singing to his flowers.

Alex also glared at me, swished his tail, and then left.

I sighed. Heavily. What was I supposed to do? I had assignments coming out of my ears, dossiers to go through, a necromancer to catch and undead to slay. And looming over all of that, I'd kissed a boy and hadn't spoken to him since.

What the Rifts are you thinking, Kat? I scolded myself. *Why haven't you messaged him?*

The answer was simple:

I didn't know what to say.

I've fought well over a hundred monsters now. Killed two people. I've banished a vampiric god, met an archdemon, befriended a pixie, and defied death more times than I could count.

Yet, I was clueless about this. I didn't even know what this was. Relationships, dating, intimacy. What was it all? What were the rules? How did I win? Could I win?

I just didn't know, and that disturbed me more than any monster.

"Kat, you need to focus," Treth said, quietly. Almost soothingly.

"How? On what?"

"On anything. No point juggling multiple balls if you're going to drop them all. Pick something, and then solve it. Then move onto the next."

I snorted. "Easier said than done."

"At least deal with one thing at a time. If Colin is on your mind…"

"Who said anything about Colin?!" I blushed a fierce red.

I could feel Treth's mischievous grin.

"I was there, you know?"

Oh, yeah. He was. Sometimes I forgot. That added another awkward thing to the mix. Treth was always with me. Even when I was wanting to get intimate with someone…

I thought that that would disturb me, but I found myself not really caring if Treth watched what I was doing. Even if it was an inappropriate situation. Treth had been with me for years now. I'd shared my most important and sensitive moments with him. We'd almost died together…so many times. Why should I care if he watched me have sex?

The final thought made me involuntarily blush. Not because of the thought of Treth watching me have sex, but that I was thinking about sex at all.

As I've said, I'm not used to this sort of thing. My inexperience is across the board, leading to me not exactly being a prude, but to being a bit scared of sexual intimacy.

Ridiculous, isn't it? With everything that I do, I'm afraid of sex. Well, not exactly sex – but everything surrounding it.

"Do you like him?" Treth asked.

"I…I think I do."

"Good enough for me. Message him."

"Now?"

"Yeah."

"We have these dossiers to go through…"

"And they aren't going anywhere. Message Colin. See if you can go to his apartment. We've never been there."

"You're awfully eager."

"Kat," Treth was suddenly serious. "I've said it before, and I say it now. The quest is important, but so is your happiness. If Colin makes you happy, then that's what I want."

I hesitated. "What about you?"

"Me? That's not really relevant."

"Sure, it is. We share a body."

"Share? It's more like I'm hitching a ride."

That was a more appropriate description.

"But, Treth…if Colin and I persist…"

"We'll cross that bridge when we get there. First, you need to make sure that Colin doesn't think you've gone dark on him."

I drew my phone like I would a weapon and considered its lock screen. I took a breath and put in my pin.

There was an unopened message from Colin. From that night:

"I enjoyed the night. Let's have another sometime."

I hadn't opened it. Much less replied.

I frowned. I hoped Colin didn't think I resented him for some stupid reason. I really didn't. I just didn't know what to do.

"Just ask if you can come over," Treth ordered, quietly. How was he better at this than me? He looked like he was my age, and I'm pretty sure that medieval Avathor didn't have a similar dating system to 21st century Earth.

I finally typed a message:

"It was great. Would like to see you. Can I come over?"

Then, I waited. A dreaded age. Seconds turned to epochs, as I watched my phone. Duer flew inside, considered speaking to me, shook his head and then went to do whatever pixies do. As millennia passed and I began hating myself for blowing my chance, my phone buzzed.

I grasped at it and checked the message.

"That'd be great! Pranish is working at my apartment. How does spaghetti bolognaise sound?"

I grinned ear to ear.

"Sounds great! I'll be there soon x."

The x was involuntary, and I kicked myself for sending it. But then Colin sent his address followed by an "x" as well. I felt a warm pang.

I stood up with new-found energy and focus. I smiled all the while putting on my salamander coat and holstering Voidshot and sheathing my seax. I wouldn't take the swords, but who knew what beast could disturb me on the way.

***

I rode my motorcycle to Colin's apartment. It was so liberating to finally not have to rely on taxis all the time. I rang the doorbell to his apartment at the front and someone buzzed me in. Colin's apartment was on the third floor. I scaled the staircase and found myself at his door. My chest was tight with trepidation and excitement. What was I going to say? What was I going to do? What did I want to do?

Finally, I knocked.

Pranish answered.

"Hey, Kats." He gave me a faint smile, but his mannerisms showed that he wanted to get back to work. "Colin's just grocery shopping. Should be back soon."

I entered and hugged my friend in greeting.

"You're awfully smiley today. Did…" A mischievous grin lit up his face. "Did something happen?"

I punched him lightly in the shoulder.

"None of your business. How are things?"

He shrugged as he made his way to his laptop. "Same old."

Colin's apartment was about the same size as mine. A bit larger, actually. There was a separate room for the kitchen. Instead of a living room area, however, he had a small dining room table, currently adorned with two laptops, scrolls, books and paperwork.

Pranish took a seat and I remained standing. I put my hands in my jean pockets to avoid fidgeting. Pranish didn't seem to notice or didn't care enough to ask.

"Seen Trudie lately?" I asked.

He bit his lip. "A bit. In class. She's lip-locked to that guy all the other times."

I frowned. "And how does that make you feel?"

Dr Drummond, Therapist.

Pranish squinted at me. "How is it meant to make me feel? Can't be helped."

He returned to his work.

"Can be helped. Just gotta do something about it."

Pranish sighed, gave up on trying to work, and looked at me.

"Do what, exactly?"

I leaned in, looking him squarely in the eyes.

"Fight for what you love, Pranish Ahuja," I said, mock seriously. I must've been in a good mood.

85

Before he could respond, Colin opened the door, carrying three bags of groceries. I immediately forgot about my conversation with Pranish and ran over.

"Hey, Kat." Colin grinned.

I leaned in to take some of the bags off him, and then stood stock still as his lips met mine. I didn't close my eyes this time. Didn't need to. It was a quick peck. I didn't manage to retrieve any bags as he jostled past and into the kitchen.

"I'm just going to get this ready. We can eat in a few years from now."

Pranish stared at me as I stood silently.

"Pffft…and you're trying to give me relationship advice."

He turned back to his computer.

I came to my senses soon after and followed Colin into the kitchen.

He was busy cutting carrots. The groceries were laid out on the counter. He had taken off his blazer and was wearing a white buttoned up shirt with its sleeves rolled up. I noted that he wasn't exactly well-built. Slender, but not muscly. I had a lot more definition, but that came with the territory.

I also noted that I liked him this way.

"So, how was work?" I asked, slowly making my way towards him.

"Work?" he said, absentmindedly. "Oh, yeah. Helped the public prosecutor with this and that."

There was an awkward pause, only filled with the sound of the knife hitting the cutting board. Thud. Thud. Thud.

Finally, I looked down, unable to take it.

"I'm sorry that I didn't message you sooner."

He looked at me and smiled faintly.

"It's fine, Kat. I'll be honest, I was a bit worried. Especially with your work and all. Pranish didn't seem worried, though, so I chalked it up to you just being busy with that Necrolord stuff."

Wait...so he didn't think I was ignoring him? My relief was palpable.

"Yeah, I had a pretty bad hunt yesterday..."

I unconsciously rubbed a bruise on my arm from when the abomination had swiped me.

Colin finished the carrots and moved onto some garlic cloves. Seemed he liked fresh ingredients in his spaghetti. I cooked instant noodles for dinner, so this would be a treat.

"Want to talk about it?" he asked.

"Not really…"

My words hung in the air. He continued working, as I stood awkwardly, my hands fidgeting behind my back.

"Do…"

What are you asking, Kat?

"Do you really like me?" I asked, my voice almost breaking. What am I? A school child.

Colin laughed. Not maliciously, but from surprise.

"Is that what you're worried about?"

He put down his knife and approached me. My heart started beating fast. Was this fear? No. But something similar.

"I do like you, Kat," he said, his eyes earnest as they stared into mine.

He took my hands and my breath caught in my throat.

"Does…this…"

Stuttering again, Kat? Really?

"Does…does this mean we're officially dating?"

He grinned. "Well, that depends. Do you want to be officially dating?"

"Yes," I said, without hesitation. That surprised me, and I felt Treth's surprise as well, followed by satisfaction.

His grin turned into a beaming smile as he hugged me, and I hugged back.

As Murphy's Law is an ironclad rule, however, my cell phone rang, and Colin released me.

"I hope that work doesn't need to take you away now," Colin said, returning to his food preparation. "You need to taste my world famous spag-bol."

I smiled at him and then frowned at my phone. The caller ID read: James Montague.

Better answer this, as much as I didn't want to.

"This is Drummond," I answered.

"Good work on that abomination yesterday," James replied.

I grunted in reply.

"I hope you're resting up."

"Hard to do, Montague." I almost snickered at my rhyme. Hey, I like puns. Sue me!

"Try to rest up, then. Drake has a lead. A stronghold. We think the Necrolord might be hiding there. We're raiding it tomorrow morning. Need you kitted out by 5am. You're on point. My men are green, and I have a feeling that no other agency hunter is gonna understand what we see in there as much as you would."

"5am? I have a class tomorrow."

"We'll sign a note for you," he replied, dully. He hung up.

"Work?" Colin asked. He was opening a packet of pasta. "I hope that 5am means you can stay for dinner."

I went over to him and kissed him on the cheek.

"It does. And if it hadn't, they would've needed to find a new hunter."

Chapter 6. The Raid

The van was dark, lit by a single red bulb overhead. The faint light let me see the expressions of my fellow passengers. Two cops, glaring at me. They were the two from the bar. They remembered my view of cops. I must say, however, after seeing the way the cops had handled themselves against the abomination, I'd gained some newfound respect for them. They'd laid down their lives. That was worth something.

Besides the cops, there were five hunters. Three from Puretide and two freelancers. They looked at me like I was a child wearing adult clothing. It didn't help that they'd been told that I was the one in charge. I had a bit of a reputation in the hunting community, but more as a side-show than as a respected hunter. Most people didn't take a part-time monster hunter very seriously.

The van went over a pothole, again, and one of the hunters hit his head on the wall. His fellow laughed and lit a cigarette. I considered stopping him, didn't want the back of the van to become a hotbox, but thought better of it. Didn't want these guys hating me any more than they did already.

All the same, I hoped that we reached our destination soon. We'd been riding in the back of the van for ages already. Beforehand, we had all been stuffed into these civilian disguised vans back in Hope City proper. James had briefed us all outside Puretide HQ as the sun slowly rose in the distance.

"Our scouts have observed living guards linked to the Europeans…" James had started.

"Seriously?" a hunter piped in.

"Not the real Europeans. A gang calling themselves the Europeans. Don't ask me why. They used to run meth under Sanguineas a year back but have since become cronies under the Necrolord. There's about ten of them patrolling the stronghold at any time. Whiteshield and police support will deal with them."

"Our role?" a Puretide sarge, with a long scar down his face from a gül, asked.

"Monster elimination." James indicated me. I stifled a yawn. I had been up until 1am with Colin. Pranish didn't need Colin's help, so we watched *No Country for Old Men*.

"Drummond here is in charge. She's to identify necromantic threats and put a stop to them. Puretide and freelancer hunters, take your cue from her."

Boy, a lot of pressure on me. No one argued, but their reluctance and confusion was palpable.

That brought us to the present, where I was sitting in the back of a dark van, with a bunch of burly men strapped with firearms staring at me. I stared right back, wearing my swords, glowing coat and my C96 Mauser pistol. We were a motley crew.

The van pulled to a stop and everyone stood.

The one cop stood at the front and drew his pistol. Other hunters did the same. I stayed at the back.

The cop put his hand on the handle of the door. You could cut the tension in the car with a knife.

Automatic gunfire rang out. We heard shouting, muffled by the walls of this metal box. A different type of gunfire joined the mix in response. A few seconds, then it was done.

The cop opened the door and we filed out.

The first thing I noted about the slums was the smell. It smelled of burnt rubber, rotting meat and trash-fire. The second: the sky was a dark grey. I had some experience with dark weylines. In my line of work, you have to go into a few of them. Necromancy necessarily corrupts weylines, after all. But I'd never been in a truly dark weyline. I thought I had. I thought that the sense of unease and toxicity in the air was the limits of the dark weyline's mundane effects on the Earth. I was wrong. The sky was choking, strangled of direct sunlight and the purifying rays of the moon and stars. The slums were coated in this thick magical smog. It was no wonder that there were no plants or trees. Just broken concrete structures and scrap shanties.

How could anything, or anyone, live in such a place?

The fact that over a million people did live in the slums of Hope City became ever more disturbing.

Whiteshield operatives and police were mopping up wounded men wearing baggy clothes bearing imagery of assorted flags of pre-Cataclysm European nations. A few of the gangsters held their hands behind their heads, knees on the ground. Policemen were setting up a perimeter, shooing away dirty bystanders, many of whom were carrying firearms openly. A Whiteshield sorcerer sparked a fireball in his hand, sending the more reluctant watchers running.

James Montague, in full navy-blue combat gear, was overlooking the clean-up. He looked our way, at the monster hunters.

"We're going to breach the front entrance," he said. "Then I want you to identify and eliminate the undead within."

We nodded and took our spaces behind the breaching team – another Whiteshield sorcerer. The sorcerer pulled his hands back, took a deep breath, and punched the door. The door exploded into splinters and the breaching team charged into the dust. I saw flashes in the dark. Heard gunshots and shouting. It reminded me of when I'd fought the vampires in the Blood Cartel. I'd had no gun then. Guy and Brett basically carried me through that situation. I drew Voidshot and my wakizashi. I wouldn't be as vulnerable now.

The gunshots stopped. I counted down. Three, two, one…

I entered after the breachers, my face-plate keeping out the worst of the dust and debris. The hunters followed. We fanned out, checking rooms and following the trail of the breachers. None of them cried out at any monsters, so we took our time.

The building was barebones. Some of the rooms didn't even have any furniture. A few gangsters lay dead in the hallways, shot peppering their chests.

We reached the breachers soon after, without any sign of our prey. James arrived behind us, bringing some police and Whiteshield operatives.

"Any undead?" he asked, quietly. I shook my head. He frowned. He really expected this place to be chock-a-block with zombies. Was his intel faulty?

"What's behind this door?" he asked the breaching team.

"About to find out," the sorcerer with something akin to geomancy or force manipulation answered.

We stood back as the sorcerer charged up his spark and punched the door, sending a shockwave that flung it off its hinges. The other breacher went in, shotgun at the ready. But he didn't fire. We filed in. One of the cops immediately started retching. Even the Puretide guys looked pale. I had seen similar sights before but couldn't help but feel the very peculiar (for me) urge to vomit.

Rows upon rows of the freshly dead, with their chests ripped open and their organs deposited into ice boxes and tanks of green goo, lay on fold-out tables, metal countertops and make-shift surgery beds. Bloodied surgery tools, ranging from genuine medical apparatus to serrated kitchen knives and hacksaws, were abandoned near the corpses.

We were on a stairway, looking down at the subterranean workshop. It was huge. Larger than the building on top. It seemed that Drake's intel wasn't that bad after all. This was a necromantic project on an industrial scale. I had seen necromancy "chop-shops" before, but this wasn't just a small little workshop run by a peculiar mage wearing dark robes. This was…

"A fucking factory," the smoking cop so eloquently put it.

"File…" James put his hand in front of his mouth. He just stopped himself from vomiting. "File in. See if you can find anything."

He turned to me as the hunters, cops and Whiteshield operatives descended and combed the area.

"What do you make of this?"

Did he really think I was an authority on this? I'm a second-year university student. Yes, I happen to hunt monsters for a living, but isn't there someone else more qualified? Even so, I gave it my best shot.

I pointed at some concentrations of collected organs. "Zombies and revenants don't need many organs. They can function on their brain and heart alone. A stomach, as well, if you want them to last longer. Flesh puppets, which the Necrolord seems to favour, don't need any organs at all."

"So, this gang was preparing corpses for the Necrolord?"

"Not exactly. Most necromancers leave the corpses as is unless they are attempting to mutate them. Zombies don't need all their organs but are hardier with them. It is also deemed unnecessary work for the creation of flesh puppets…"

"You seem to know a lot about how necromancers think…" James said, with just a bit of accusation in his voice.

I looked him dead in the eyes. "Don't dare imply that I've got some necromantic interest in me, James. I'll readily kill a necromancer just as readily as I'd kill their servants. I learn about them, so I can effectively kill them."

He nodded. He knew my track record. Knew that I wasn't just blustering. Then why did he test me?

"Sorry. Go on…"

I nodded, acknowledging his apology, and continued.

"It is just conjecture, but…every empire requires capital. The Necrolord has established an extensive network of gangs. Not so different from an empire. Fear can only take one so far. She must be paying her living servants something. An incentive, or a subsistence wage."

I looked again at the organs, so haphazardly stacked in their containers and table tops – like discarded meat at a butcher.

"I suspect that she is funding her campaign with organ trafficking. She harvests her victims for organs, uses what is left for her experimentation and army building, and then sells the organs to fund her empire. Put some detectives on it and I am confident that they'll find that I am correct."

James nodded, impassive, but with just a hint of respect hidden behind his strong cop façade.

We turned to re-examine the factory and I immediately noticed something peculiar.

Necromancers don't only reanimate corpses. They mess with them. They shape them to their whims.

And sometimes, a walking corpse isn't the worst thing a necromancer may put in your way.

A bloated corpse, as if it had been waterlogged, lay just in the centre of the factory floor. A cop was moving towards it. Too close.

I cried out. He didn't respond, so I leapt over the railing, doing a number on my still recovering knees, and rushed towards him.

Too late.

The corpse exploded.

Chapter 7. Miasma

I saw black shapes as I opened my eyes, my head screaming, and my vision blurred. I felt things in me. Sharp things. All over. My legs, my shoulders, my arms. I had turned at the last minute, letting my salamander coat take the brunt of the damage, but I still got pegged by a barrage of bone. Only the miasma that followed gave me a short respite from the pain in my everywhere. I could only be thankful that my lungs felt okay, except for the searing pain of the corruption gas caught in my throat.

I took stock of what I remembered before I blacked out. The cop ignored me, or didn't hear me, and brushed right up against the bloated corpse. It wriggled violently and exploded before most could react. It had been filled with shards of bone. Like a sack. Following the bone came the miasmic gas. We should've been wearing respirators, but I wasn't even sure that would've worked. Corruption magic was potent. It seldom cared about mundane things like gas masks.

My vision was still hazy, but I was awake. In excruciating pain, but awake. I still couldn't move. Too weak. And I didn't really want to move. If I was in this much pain now, how much pain would I be in if I moved?

"Kat?" Treth asked. I tried to open my mouth to respond but couldn't. I must still be held in the grips of the miasma.

The black shapes approached and I felt fear. I normally faced my fear by charging at it. But I couldn't charge at it now.

My hearing, which I noticed now had been silenced, returned. I heard footsteps. Not the natural and melodic footfalls of the living, but the calculated and jagged steps of the undead.

Well, what else did I expect? A pack of dwarves?

As my hearing had returned, so did my vision, revealing the visage of the wight, only a handspan away.

Feeling returned to my arms as the miasma dissipated from me. I reached for my sword, despite the pain, and then cried out as intense cold froze my hands onto the floor. They were stuck in shards of ice. I already felt the freezing pain in my bones. If I was stuck like this for too long, I'd lose my hands to frostbite.

"No need to struggle," the wight rasped, cocked his head. "Kat Drummond."

The way he said my name sent me chills that outperformed the ice around my hands. He said my name like he was contemplating it. That he wasn't sure what to think about it. If he should consider me prey, a pebble, a child, or a toy.

"I…" he backed away and gave a flourishing bow. I heard his bones creak. "Am Frederico DeSantos. My mistress calls me the Marshal."

He cocked his head again. "I enjoy that title and ask that you refer to me the same."

He was much more eloquent now, but still had that ancient rasp to his every word. Was like trying to articulate through sandpaper. He turned to the rest of the occupants of the room. They were still comatose. Those who were still breathing. The others lay peppered with bone-shot, eviscerated.

"Your compatriots are still under my mistress's spell. She told me that you would be able to awaken from it more easily than they. Even so, I disenchanted you as I entered."

I glanced side to side, trying to take stock of my surroundings and to ignore the shards of bone lodged all over my body. The flesh puppets were ignoring my living allies, rather collecting the abandoned organs in their containers. The Necrolord must not worry about access to corpses, but organs cost money.

"Why?" I finally asked, trying to hide my fear and loathing, and failing.

"Why…did I awake you?"

"Why haven't you killed me?"

A lipless, horrific grin crossed the Marshal's face.

"My mistress…"

He considered his words.

"…doesn't wish for you to die."

"Yet?"

"Ever."

That was a surprise.

"She considers you her greatest ally, Kat Drummond."

"Greatest ally?!" I spat. The thought made me sick. "Fuck off to your hole. And take your mistress with you."

His grin didn't abate.

"I stay my hand, Kat Drummond, for love of my mistress. She has plans for you. It is my job to ensure that while you are involved in her downfall, that you fail to defeat her, while also failing to die."

"Seems convoluted. Kill me."

"Kat…" Treth whined. He didn't like that idea.

"Not until my mistress orders me to do so."

"You're a wight, aren't you?" I changed the topic. If I couldn't kill it, and it wasn't going to kill me, I might as well learn something.

"I am," he said, matter of factly.

"Yet you follow a master. That is rare among your kind. Why?"

"Why do we follow anyone?" he countered. "For passion, for pride, as a means to an end."

He cocked his head, considering his words. I got the impression that English wasn't his first language. He had to think things through before trying to articulate them through his dead lack of lips. I'd say it was a miracle that he could speak at all, but necromancy is more proof that miracles don't exist. Only machinations.

"My mistress is a *visionário*. She sees what can be. She fights for it, despite the odds."

"She's a murderous psychopath."

"Judge not what you don't understand." His grin was gone. "Only know that you survive because she admires you. She wants to work with you. While you may not know it yet, there is another enemy lurking in the shadows. A common foe."

"My foe is the undead and those who bring them into the world." I said my point with an unarguable finality.

"You sure like to play dangerously," Treth commented, but I felt unmistakable pride from my spirit companion.

"You will learn," the Marshal said, simply. "You will learn why I serve. And you will come to be allies with my mistress. She knows this, so I know this."

"Fuck off," I said, just as simply, if more eloquently.

The Marshal turned his back on me, his hand on the pommel of his rapier.

"I aim to keep you alive, Kat Drummond, but the best way to do that is to ensure that you are unable to threaten my mistress further. Hopefully, those bone shards hit nothing vital, but will keep you in a hospital bed for a while."

I contemplated swearing at him again, but he left. The ice melted, and I considered charging him, but as I moved towards him, I fell. Blackness took me.

Chapter 8. Again and Again

If you aren't already, get used to me waking up in hospital beds. What I needed to get used to, however, is waking up with Colin sitting by my side, a look of feigned calm on his face, hiding distress. I blinked the sleep out of my eyes. I no longer felt the excruciating pain of the Necrolord's bloated corpse trap. But I still felt weak.

Colin smiled, weakly, as I awoke. He reached for my hand and I grasped it. My skin still felt a bit numb, but at least I still had my hands. The frost was just a painful memory now.

"You're awake," he said, matter-of-factly.

"Yeah," I said.

His face was passive. His usually laid-back persona. But I saw a pain behind his eyes. A tremor to his lip.

"Second time," he said. Second time he'd seen me in the hospital.

"Yeah, it happens a lot. I'm used to it. I'll be fine."

He nodded, slowly. I tightened my grip on his hand. He was staying impassive. Staying cool. But his lip was quivering, and I saw moisture in his eyes.

I did this to him.

I'd hurt him, if not directly, but through my relationship with him. I was going to get hurt, and that hurt him.

I didn't want to hurt him. But I knew that I'd do it again.

In some ways, I'm selfish. I wanted Colin, but I also knew that I needed to keep hunting. It was more than my life.

All I could do was be more careful next time.

"What does the monster look like now, Kat?" I heard the one voice I didn't want to hear. Andy. He entered, just behind Colin's chair. His hands were nonchalantly in his pockets. He looked dishevelled. His hair was a mess. There was a thin layer of black lipstick stained on his lips. He could've wiped it off, but I got the impression that he wanted us to know what he'd been doing.

"Rather not talk about it," I said, as diplomatically as I could. I didn't want to hurt Colin any further with the details.

"Nah, go on," Andy said. His tone was jokey, but his expression was something else. Not exactly nonchalant. More intense. Almost predatory.

I ignored him. He approached. I'd hadn't liked Andy for months, but I couldn't help but feel more than disdain for him as he drew closer. I felt an overwhelming menace exude from my one-time crush.

"Why not, Kat? You're a monster hunter. A real badass. Talk shop."

"Not now," I hissed. Colin was avoiding eye contact, looking at the sheets of the hospital bed.

Andy considered me, and then looked at Colin. It was brief, but I caught a glimpse of a snarl.

"Is it because of this pussy? He too much of a wimp to listen about monsters?"

"You're the fucking coward!" I shouted, all attempts at diplomacy gone. The exertion hurt my chest, but my anger numbed the pain.

Andy's head snapped towards me. He was no longer wearing his impassive mask, but he also no longer held his air of menace. He looked aghast. More than stung. He looked like a scolded dog.

"Get out," I said, much more quietly and much colder. His expression descended further. He was distraught. He turned his back to us and half ran out. Trudie entered as he left, giving him a concerned and confused stare.

She looked at me, staring daggers.

"What the fuck was that?"

"He started it…" I muttered.

Trudie raised her hand to stop me from continuing. Colin looked about to speak up, but Trudie's expression, deep-breath taking, and closed eyes did not allow for interruption.

"You promised to be nice," she finally said.

I opened my mouth to argue, but she interrupted me again.

"He's my boyfriend, Kat. If you can't get over him and have to shout at him for stupid reasons because you're jealous, then we can't hang out anymore. I'm sorry, but I have to go."

Trudie promptly left – probably into the arms of that jerk that I was sickened to have ever thought that I liked.

As the silence settled, I tightened my grip again on Colin's hand.

"He's wrong, you know?"

Colin looked me in the eyes. He'd been crying, just quietly enough that we hadn't noticed. I knew it had nothing to do with Andy's bullying, however. Colin had been teetering on the edge for a while. He had found out that he could lose me. That thought simultaneously filled me with warmth and an intense guilt.

"You're a hundred times the man than he'll ever be," I said. Colin didn't respond. Despite my sincerity, I don't think he agreed.

Chapter 9. Insecurity

Colin visited me every day as I recovered. Pranish visited once or twice but was anxious to get back to his work. Trudie didn't come again but did email my missed notes to my laptop (which Colin brought to the hospital, so I could keep busy). We were having a fight, brought on by her jerk of a boyfriend, but we were still friends. Just needed to let things cool off. We'd gone through worse. Did I ever tell you when I slipped and broke her PlayStation?

Conrad visited as well, arguing with Cindy if he wasn't playing on his cell phone. He was thoroughly addicted. Brett also popped in. Apparently, Drakenbane had been hired by the Council to join the Necrolord case. He suspected that he would be under my command when I recovered. He didn't say 'if' I recovered. He knew I would. I didn't know what to think about giving orders to Brett. Sure, I'd told him what to do in the past – but this time he would have to listen.

James Montague, who had also been hospitalised for some smaller injuries, popped in as well, accompanied by Drake. Updates on Necrolord action, casualty reports, weyline decay, stolen corpses. Everything. It was too much. Too much to process and too much to cope with without the catharsis of killing something that was already dead.

In the absence of visitors, Treth and I pondered our situation. We reviewed what we knew. That the Necrolord liked me, for some reason, that she found great joy in toying with me, and that she had warned me about enemies in the shadows.

I would have ignored such words from an undead and their master normally, but someone that I trusted (even if I shouldn't really trust a demon) had warned me about enemies in the shadows already. While I could not be sure of its nature, I was beginning to suspect the third force in all of this.

"What do you make of it?" I asked Treth, whispering so that the nurses wouldn't hear me.

"Deceit by the necromancer," he suggested, but I heard doubt in his voice. "Or a genuine warning carrying an ulterior motive. The necromancer may be telling the truth. There may be a third-party, but they may not be our enemy. Or they might."

"What I can't help feeling is that there may be a connection. The necromancer worked with the Blood Cartel, then went her separate ways from them. What if the Blood Cartel is still functioning?"

"Vampires seldom die. I am sure that the Blood Cartel is still alive. I am also quite sure if the enemy was the Blood Cartel, that the necromancer would say so. She readily gave up that information once before."

"So, someone else?" I pondered. "Perhaps, Digby's clients? The person on the phone."

"Perhaps. That would also link to the warning from the archdemon."

I frowned. "I don't like this. The undead are meant to be simple. We go in. We slay. We get out. The investigations are meant to be for mimics, spirits and demons. Not the undead."

"At least we're closing in. It's better than watching the Necrolord eat the city from afar."

I nodded, grimly. We weren't making much headway, but at least we were on the case.

I heard a knock on the door. Colin entered.

"Talking to someone?" he asked.

I smiled. "Just thinking aloud."

He nodded. "I heard you're being discharged today."

"Yep. Can leave now, actually…"

"Would you like a lift?"

Of course, I would. That was a no-brainer. I'm a frugal girl, and free lifts are free. But something made me hesitate at accepting. Some sort of subconscious anticipation and fear at such an anticipation. Not the sort of bad terror, but that natural anxiety you get from pondering something new.

Colin had lifted me many times before, so what was this anxiety?

"It's fine if you'd like to be alone…" Colin said, raising his hands diplomatically, and a bit nervously.

"No, no," I interrupted, a bit too loudly. "A lift would be great. Thanks."

I gave him a nervous grin, and then asked for some privacy as I got ready to leave the hospital.

***

We didn't speak on the way home. My fault. Colin was his usual forthcoming self. A great conversationalist. But I was stuck in brooding thought. On the periphery of my

116

mind was the Necrolord but taking centre-stage was a different type of contemplation. Something I didn't understand, even though I thought I had sorted it out. It was part excitement, part apprehension, part trepidation.

As Colin walked me to my door, I felt a searing sensation in my gut. It told me that I was at the Rubicon. Across it, potential joy and potential heartache. Behind it, more of the dark path that I already knew too well – with no hint of light.

I don't know why, but I felt that I needed to do something.

"Colin…" I murmured. "Do…do…"

I was stuttering almost as badly as he used to. And James Montague expected me to lead the crack team to eliminate a necromancer warlord? What a joke.

"Do...you…"

He came closer and squeezed my hand. I was looking at my shoes and examined his as he came into view. Sneakers. He must have not gone to court today.

I felt his hand on my cheek and looked up. The warm glow in his eyes helped me make my decision.

I took a deep breath.

"Would you like…to come in?"

He nodded, wordlessly, and I turned to open the door. Alex greeted us. Duer flew down to greet me, saw Colin, glowed a bright gold, and then disappeared into his birdhouse. I felt Treth's presence, looming over me. He was curious.

I closed the door behind us. I pondered if I should lock it or not. What message would that send? Would it send a message at all?

Stop being silly, Kat! I told myself. I locked it. Security and all that. He could unlatch it himself if he wanted to leave. He wasn't a prisoner.

I turned to see Colin examining my apartment and felt an intense embarrassment. My apartment was a mess. Of course, it was! I could expect Trudie to look after Alex, but not to clean my apartment. Especially seeing that we were fighting.

He didn't say a word, however, and I suddenly felt the urge to get sick from anxiety. What was I doing to myself? Was this really worth it? What was I even trying to do?

"I need to…excuse me…"

I didn't wait for his reply as I entered the bathroom. I closed the door behind me and made a beeline for the basin. I submerged my head under the water, to clean my angst away. To shock my system out of nausea.

A drenched girl with bags under her eyes, and a mess of dark chestnut hair stared back at me in the mirror. I bit my lip, and so did she. She had scars. On the side of her head, her neck, and her cheek. Above her cleavage were welts. Healed, but a permanent reminder of her ordeals. I had more scars than that. Too many to count. From wraiths, from zombies, from ghouls, from traps and accidents. Healing magic could only take one so far. I was left with a reminder of every time I had barely escaped death.

And that was it.

The reason for my anxiety. The reason why I so desperately wanted Colin to stay the night.

I was going to die. Probably soon. And I needed to do more before that happened.

But could I even do it? Would he want to do it?

I looked at myself in the mirror, a canvas of wounds that I'd never cared about until now. I felt tears well up in my eyes.

"Stop that," Treth said, almost forcefully, but with a sincere concern.

"What was I thinking?" I whispered, even though Colin might hear me in the other room.

"You were realising that there's something as important, if not more, than the crusade."

I shook my head. "But it's too late for me. How can he love this?"

I indicated my reflection. I pictured the scars on the rest of my body. The ones I'd become so accustomed to while showering. I realised how abhorrent they were now. Colin was hurt when I almost died. How would he feel when he saw all this? These manifestations of every time I'd brushed up against death.

"I will say this once, Kat. And that is because I care about you enough that I will insult you for your own good."

He took in a deep breath.

"Stop being so fucking stupid."

I was stunned. Treth never swore. Well, not anytime that I can remember. And while he may have questioned my methods, he'd never called me stupid before.

Despite all that, I felt my anxiety start to dissipate. The uncertainty did remain, however.

"I don't know how to do this, Treth. I don't even know if I want to."

"Realise that you CAN do what you want, and then do it. You're holding yourself back."

"What…what if he doesn't like what he sees?"

"Then he doesn't deserve you. You're beautiful."

I was too stunned to respond. Treth had never said something like this before. I didn't know how to respond. He continued, his tone becoming serious and quiet.

"And if it is about…me, being there…you don't need to worry."

"It's not…" I tried to argue but realised that part of it was. I wasn't sure what I wanted, but it wasn't helping that I had Treth over my shoulder. I felt that I had to make decisions that were best for both of us. Having sex in front of him wasn't my idea of supporting the team.

"I can actually seclude myself," Treth said. "There is a place I go when I need solitude. When I feel that you need some alone time. I go there…during your more sensitive times."

So, Treth had never actually seen me naked? I thought he was just coyly shutting his eyes, maybe sneaking a peak. But if he could cloister himself in some spectral chamber, that meant that…I could be alone with myself again. Or alone with someone else.

"I'm going to go away now. For a bit. When you…need me again, just call me."

Before I could respond, I felt Treth disappear. It was the same feeling I had when he was silent for a long time, but with the knowledge of his chamber, I now felt his absence distinctly. In a way, it was uncomfortable, but also liberating. I could call him again, when I missed him, but it let me be myself, without fear of at least one person's judgement.

I looked in the mirror. Nothing had changed, but I felt different.

Beautiful.

My cheeks warmed, but I smiled. If only faintly.

"Are you okay?" I heard Colin's sincere concern from the other side of the door.

"Yes," I said, and opened it. Colin smiled, but I still noticed a hint of his worry. He let me pass and I stood there shyly for just a second before making my way to the couch. Luckily, Colin followed without my prompting. Phew!

He sat next to me.

My chest was tight. I sat with my arms held tightly against my sides. I considered my lap.

How did I proceed? What was I meant to do?

Colin wasn't doing anything either. Did I misjudge him? Was he so afraid of losing me that he was reconsidering this whole dating thing?

Stop being stupid, I told myself. It could have just as easily been Treth saying it.

I looked at Colin and tried to decipher his thoughts. He looked concerned, worried, nervous, shy. I got the weird thought in my head that he may be feeling the same way as I was. That, despite our initial minor confession, we still didn't trust in our own or each other's feelings.

But I did like him. I knew I did. And I knew that if I was going to die, then there were some things I wanted to do.

I took a deep breath. A punctuation on my nerves. A conclusive gesture that told me that I had made up my mind.

I shifted my weight and felt the warmth of his thigh as we touched. He looked into my eyes, and I saw the twin signs of nerves and anticipation. At least, that's what I thought I saw. Don't take my observations of people as gospel. I'm not a psychologist. Or even a well-rounded twenty-year-old.

I leaned my face towards his and felt the warmth of his breath. I noted that he was breathing nervously. So was I. We were both still young. And so oddly similar. Was he as inexperienced as I? That thought made me feel a bit more comfortable. Comfortable enough to do what I did next.

My lips met his. He was anticipating me, but I still felt his initial shock. Then, he reciprocated.

Through the process, our arms found their way around each other, and I found myself on his lap. Our lips only separated for moments apiece. We were making up for lost time. I was preparing in case this never happened again.

I stopped kissing him, and he leaned back. His face was flushed, but he looked happy. Seeing that filled me with some of the cleanest joy I'd felt in a long time.

Was it time? I asked myself. I blushed at the thought.

I was straddling Colin's lap. It felt right. The closeness. But going further. I didn't know…

Colin leaned closer towards me and put his mouth near my ear. His breath sent a pleasurable shiver down my spine.

"Don't rush," he said, some uncertainty in his own voice, but with sincerity. "Only when you really want to."

His words made me calm. Genuinely. I no longer felt that acidity of trepidation. There was only the joy of the moment. I engulfed him in my arms, scarred as they may be, and our lips reunited.

Chapter 10.   Leads

The glares from the hunters weren't any better than the reception I got at the flesh factory before my hospitalisation. It was a new crowd. No cops. No Whiteshield. Just Drakenbane and Puretide, with a few freelancers. Fellow monster hunters. Heavy-hitters. Heavy-hitters being forced to take orders from a twenty-year-old girl. As you might guess – they didn't like it one bit.

We'd rendezvoused at an underground parking garage in a border slum. James Montague was there, as was to be expected, and so was Drake. A bunch of agency and freelance hunters were loitering, smoking and checking their guns. I had hoped that there'd be some more close-combat specialists. Undead can shrug off a lot of firepower. It takes a clean cut or a decisive and destructive blow to the head to put them down effectively.

I also saw Brett, smoking away while joking with some other Drakenbane agents that I'd never met. Seeing him now shouldn't have sparked anything. I used to find the guy irritating but, through some tribulations, I'd come to like him. Not like-like. Or did I? No, I liked Colin. I was certain of that. But seeing Brett now, especially after my night with Colin, confused me.

Despite my confusion and awkwardness, I greeted Brett cordially. He introduced me to some Drakenbane agents, a guy named Tod and another named Busani. They didn't know what to make of me. Before we could proceed, James spoke loudly to the assembled group.

"Anti-personnel units have already been deployed at the site. Your job is extermination. Get in the vans and get ready to deploy. Positively identify the target and kill on sight. Questions?"

A man wearing a Puretide logo put up his hand.

"None? Good." James ignored him and entered one of the vans. Everyone lined up to file into each vehicle.

"Hey," Brett whispered, as I was about to step into my van. "They do anything stupid and you tell me, right?"

I didn't know what he was talking about, but I nodded all the same.

My head wasn't really in the game. I was thinking about my night with Colin, and the confusion I had over Brett wasn't helping. Colin hadn't gone further, and I was okay with that. We had done more than I'd ever done before. And I'd enjoyed it.

"I'm glad I didn't go all the way," I had told Treth after Colin had left. "It means I won't die yet."

"Weird logic, but okay," Treth said. He didn't really want to hear about my night. Understandable.

It was weird logic, however. And I knew it wasn't true. All that night meant was that I had something to lose. And someone to lose me. Could I really be doing this again? Could I really risk hurting Colin again?

And as much as there was a sense of profound happiness in doing what I did, there was that inevitable regret. The thought that I was taking this too fast, that I was falling in love too fast, and that if anything was to happen to me, that I was just causing pain to more and more people.

I'm not a well-adjusted girl. Can you blame me? My parents died in front of me when I was eight. I'd be odder if I was fine after that. And while I maintained friendships with my childhood friends, I seldom made more. I kept people at a distance. There was a reason I lived alone, despite the expense. People were things to be hurt. I didn't want to hurt people.

But I had invited Colin into my life. For good and ill, he was here to stay.

But did that mean I had to choose between Colin or the crusade? Could I?

That was a distraction right now, however. I needed to focus. On the job at hand. On Treth's *crusade*. Despite the disrespect that the other hunters had for me, I had a job to do. To lead them. To slay monsters. I needed to be thinking straight for this.

The van shook as we drove over a series of potholes. Slum roads again. I bit my lip, thankful for my face-plate that would hide my nerves. Last time I'd been on the job, the stench and dark sky had been just an unpleasant taster to the true abhorrent sights within.

What would we find this time?

Another flesh factory? An undead horde? The necromancer herself? So many possibilities. I didn't know which I found more terrifying.

But I'd faced worse before. I'd face this.

The van lurched to a stop. I took a deep breath.

Light burst into the van as the back door opened. James Montague greeted us, wearing a respirator with his combat gear.

"We've *incapacitated* the human targets." He looked at me. "Your job now. We've got reliable reports of undead near and in this building."

"Sarge," a freelance hunter tagging along with Puretide piped up. To my knowledge, Montague wasn't a sergeant. "Why the chick?"

"The *chick* is your boss. You listen to her, you get out okay, and get paid."

"How old is she?" another hunter added.

"Doesn't fucking matter," Brett bellowed, exiting the van he'd been stationed in.

James glared at the Drakenbane hunter, but the menace in Brett's voice already silenced the man.

"So, everyone said their piece? Good. Get moving. Purge the place. Find the whereabouts of the Necrolord. Hey, we might get lucky. She could be hiding in this trash-pile."

The trash-pile was a large trash-pile indeed. While it wasn't that bad, it still held that stink of burnt rubber and

130

decay. It had no windows. Just a three-storey corrugated iron behemoth, covered in rust. It may have been a clean metal grey in the past. Now, it looked like a leper, covered in rusty sores. It looked like the undead it allegedly contained.

Would I find the Necrolord within? And what would I do when I did? Was I ready to kill again?

The quickness of the answer shocked me:

Yes.

The hunters all considered me. So, did James. I examined them. I wasn't leadership material. I only just got a boyfriend. People skills weren't my forte. But this was my job now.

"Let's go," I said, simply. It must have been sufficiently compelling, as the hunter's covered their distaste and filed to the door of the corrugated structure.

"And everyone put on your respirators," I said, almost as an after-thought. "The Necrolord's MO is miasmic gas. A gas mask may not be fool proof, but it might save your life."

Pained as they looked to be listening to me, they put their masks on. I'm not sure how effective they'd be, magic is unpredictable, but it was better than nothing. And one should wear facial protection against the undead anyway. Necro-blood was hazardous.

I'm not a trained tactician, but I've hunted enough undead and observed enough combat drills to know a bit about storming a building.

"Any force and metal mages?" I asked the group, as we advanced on the double doors of the structure in a chaotic formation. Some of the hunters were talking to their friends. One of them was wearing his respirator around his neck, a cigarette in his mouth.

"Force. Wizard," a small mousy looking man with light stubble said. Not mousy. More like a hamster. He was wearing a magic school robe underneath a bulletproof vest. A freelancer. New. Probably. That'd explain his deference.

"Take point. Brett, and…" I pointed at another guy with a shotgun. "Right behind him. Any zoms charge out, put them down."

"We know how to do our jobs," the unnamed shotgunner said.

"Then do it," I countered, bluntly.

The group loitered as the mage prepared his breaching spell. Brett and the other shotgunner stood behind him, weapons ready. The mage was crouching, so they'd be able to fire over his head. The rest of the group were idling behind us. They weren't taking things very seriously. Must've thought that any mission run by a girl my age wasn't worth taking seriously. Didn't matter now, as long as they performed when the zombies started pouring out.

"In position? Good. On three."

The mage cracked his knuckles and started chanting under his breath.

"One."

Brett checked the chamber of his shotgun again.

"Two."

One of the loiterers dropped his cigarette onto the floor and stomped it out.

"Three."

The door shot forward down the hallway, more effective than any shotgun blast. Too bad there was nothing behind it. Just a dark hallway. A very dark hallway. I could barely see a few metres past the door.

"Sham mission," a Puretide agent said, lighting another cigarette.

"Getting paid. Sham or no sham. Shut up," a fellow Puretide guy with a pistol and hand-axe (which I appreciated) responded.

"The target is smart," I said. The hunters looked at me quizzically. The mage looked a bit frightened. First job, probably. The reason for the look must've been the cold edge to my voice. I got it when I was getting really deep into the hunt.

I drew my dual swords.

"I'll take point. Shotgunners by my side. I want someone with a melee weapon pulling up the rear. Tight formation. If we get jumped, don't give them any openings."

The coldness in my voice sent them into formation. The hand-axe guy drew his weapons and stood at the rear. The others formed a motley formation in between us.

"Lights on," I ordered. "They've got night-sight. We don't."

I turned on the flashlight adjoined to the side of my faceplate. Another of Pranish's upgrades before he was totally consumed by his lawmancy project.

The hallway was muggy. The metal trapped the heat from the outside and even more heat from some internal source. The darkness and tightness of the walls caused intense claustrophobia. At least it forced the hunters into a tight formation. I couldn't be sure they'd have listened to me otherwise.

"Any shield spells?" I asked, as we entered the hall and began our advance.

"Yes, sarge," the Puretide guy who'd called James *sarge* said. He said the title with an unmistakable hint of mockery.

"Get them on the front and rear."

"Right-o."

I felt a layer of coolness surround me. I didn't hear any spells. Must be a sorcerer. He'd be channelling his spark to keep the shields up. Normally, a sorcerer would complain about expending such resources. The fact that he didn't, meant he must have quite a heavy magical reserve. No wonder he was cockier than a jockey with a unicorn.

With the shield spell on me, I felt safer moving at a cautious pace down the hall. The formation followed, our boots crunching on the crusty cement flooring. Weapons and kit clicked and tapped as their owners moved. Slowly. Steadily.

"Faster, please," a hunter said. "I want to get lunch."

"Ssshhh," Brett said. He didn't need to. I can handle brats. I used to babysit.

We reached the end of the hallway and were met with a crossroads. I looked both ways. The glow of my coat, elevated by my will, and the flashlight provided a small cone of vision, but there was something unnatural about this darkness. My light stopped just too short.

"Why so scared, girly? It's just zombies. Slice and dice them," someone from the back said.

I heard Brett turn, but he sensed my apprehension and stopped.

"What is it, Kat?"

"The dark…it's moving."

The group became audibly unnerved. I heard those who hadn't drawn their weapons yet, do so. Even heard the hiss of a fireball ignite in a sorcerer's hand. The cops must've been paying a fortune for this raid to have this many magic-users on board.

Brett levelled his shotgun towards the right-hand morass of darkness.

"I can't see anything," he said. His flashlight's illumination stopped just short of where it should.

"Exactly, the dark is pressing in."

"Afraid of the dark?" someone piped up.

I ignored him.

"We stick together and go left. Watch the rear."

I proceeded before any more wise guys would try to tease me again. I didn't really care, but it was unnecessary noise. Very unprofessional.

The dark abated, just a bit, as we pressed on. But I couldn't help but have the feeling that the light we cast just didn't go as far as it should.

The hallways twisted the further we went. More and more forks. Tighter hallways, but all seemingly identical. The darkness did not decrease. It was oppressive. I kept a cool head, but I could sense everyone's nerves on a knife edge. We needed a contact soon. Every second we didn't slay something, we forgot that we could. And every moment longer that we trod along in the dark, we allowed the dark mysticism to seep into our cores, pushing out our hardened training and professional arrogance.

The sight of pallid flesh and a hunched creature just beyond the intensity of our lights made me stop. Its giggle sent a chill up my spine. It sounded like a child.

The shotgunner fired, lighting up the hallway and sending a harsh bang reverberating through the metal halls and in our ears. The creature giggled again and disappeared into the black. I felt someone trying to bustle past me. I held up my arm and only the involuntary ignition of my coat stopped the assailant.

"What the fuck? That's the target. Let's go!"

"That's an undead. A trap," I said. "If they were the target, we wouldn't be meeting them here. Maintain the formation. If we're going into a trap, we need to be on our guard."

The hunter looked at me, perplexed. "The target is there. It's just a fucking undead. Who the hell put you in charge?"

"The employers," Brett hissed.

I nodded. "Exactly. And for good reason. How many zombies have you killed?"

"Three," he said it like it was something to be proud of.

I leaned in and looked him in the eyes. He wasn't wearing a faceplate. I hoped the cold eyeless gaze from mine would unnerve him.

"I've killed 564." That was a lie. I've probably killed more.

That silenced him. He fell back in line.

"There's something ahead," Treth said. I couldn't respond without looking mad. "I see a speck of light in the distance."

"There's something ahead," I echoed Treth's words. "Get ready for combat."

I heard clicks and the intake of breath. We pressed on.

As Treth had said, there was a light. It grew closer as we advanced. The darkness didn't give way as much as I felt it should, but we soon found ourselves in a dimly lit atrium.

Unlike the labyrinth of sweltering metal hallways, this atrium was cool. Pleasant. It also looked lived in. It had a table with a bowl of half-eaten cereal on it, un upturned chair and an unmade single bed.

Was this the home of the Necrolord? Such a humble, almost depressing arrangement. I imagined them living in luxury. Twisted, evil luxury, but luxury all the same. This wasn't the type of place I expected my adversary to live in.

"Fan out. Secure the room," I said.

"For what fucking point?" the hunter from before swore.

I ignored him and walked to the half-eaten cereal bowl. Multi-coloured. Sugary. Soggy. But not too soggy. It was fresh.

"There's no other way out of this room," another hunter said.

"We went the wrong fucking way. Should've let me go after the target!"

I ignored him and leaned closer. The teaspoon was plastic. One of those teaspoons that change colour when you get it wet. Its handle was pink, and its bowl was blue.

"Are you even fucking listening?"

I heard him step towards me and felt Treth about to warn me. He stopped.

"You her fucking boyfriend?" the hunter asked.

Brett stood in his way, arms by his side. Tense.

"Cut the shit," he said. It was more menacing than his tone back at the meet.

"She fucked up the mission," the hunter said, and tried to shove Brett out the way to get to me. Before he could do so, Brett punched him square in the jaw, knocking his respirator into his teeth and chipping them.

Before anyone could intervene, the roof caved in. People cried out. I dived under the table. That allowed me the moments I needed to figure out what was going on.

Zombies. A horde of them. They'd dropped through the roof. And they were attacking the crew. Pale, writhing flesh. Naked, with their genitalia waving around. It wasn't sexual. Wasn't even funny. It was horrific. Human form twisted until it was nothing but monstrous.

The crew were too shocked to act. The force wizard managed to get off a shockwave that knocked a few zombies back, but more pressed in. Brett, his hand bleeding from punching the hunter, fired his shotgun one handed into the horde. The zombies shrugged it off. Only the hand axeman was having some joy, but his axe embedded itself into each zombie. Too slow.

I burst out from under the table, dual swords in an arc. I sliced low, sending two zoms to the floor where I impaled their heads on my blades. Quick stab. A zombie singed itself on the back of my coat. I drew my blades from their head sheathes and spitted the zombie behind me and another in front.

I never let my blade lie idle for more than a moment. A slice here. A beheading there. Twin strikes to behead one zom, his body kicked into his fellows, sending them onto the floor.

With every kill, I grew faster. My momentum increased. I didn't grow tired. I grew more excited. More comfortable. The kill came naturally to me. And with every drop of spilt necro-blood, I came to relish the hunt even more.

This was a dance. My dance. A pirouette, and zombie heads fell to the ground. A duck and slice low, and more zoms were incapacitated. If the crew didn't put them down, I did with a quick skewering or a heavy stomp to the head, sending brains and blood all over the concrete.

And with every kill, I felt ever more alive.

I knew then that I couldn't abandon this. Not for Trudie. Not even for Colin. Not for anyone. I belonged here.

The horde whittled away and as the final zombie's head fell, I singed its blood off my blades on the sleeves of my coat.

The crew stared at me, dumbstruck. Even Brett. He was panting. Red-faced. He looked proud, but even a bit afraid.

A hunter, one who had been trying to get a rise from me earlier, lay clutching his arm. The bite on his forearm was festering. Black. The necromancer's touch was still active through the zombies. He'd turn – soon.

"I don't want to die," he cried. He wore a Puretide vest. He knew what the bite meant. Tears cascaded down his cheeks, mingling with black blood smears and sweat.

His compatriot, a fellow Puretide agent, was also crying. He was unloading his revolver to put in a special bullet. Puretide had a tradition among its soldiers. When someone got bit, their fellow put them down – with a bullet with their name on it.

I rushed to the scene.

"Nobody's dying on my mission!" I yelled.

"He's bit," the Puretide agent with the revolver said, levelling it at his friend. The man clutching his infected arm started screaming.

"We've got time."

"Listen to her," Brett said. His tone brooked no disagreement.

I sheathed my dusack and held my wakizashi to my cloak. I willed the flames to heat it as fast and as hot as possible. My cloak flared up and those around me recoiled.

"Get a tourniquet ready. And some stimulants. Any of you a healer? Get a healing spell on him as soon as I'm done."

"What are you…"

Before he could finish the sentence, I grabbed the wounded man's hand, straightened his arm, and brought my sword down on the joint. He screamed as blood sprayed, the heat of my blade not being enough to cauterize the wound. Two of the hunters sent golden waves towards him and Brett leaned in with a tourniquet. He tightened it around the stump. Some blood leaked out. Only red. No black.

He was safe. None of the infection had spread.

I breathed a sigh of relief. The man had stopped screaming but was still sobbing. The rest of the crew only stared at me. Dumbstruck. It wasn't like the stares from before. Not at all.

I didn't examine them. I exited the trashed atrium, with all its clues crushed by the zombies. I re-entered the darkness.

Another battle won. But we weren't any closer to winning the war.

Chapter 11. Geese

Every time we thought we were on the Necrolord's trail, she proved three steps ahead of us. A stronghold, filled with zombies, almost burnt over our heads as we thought we were closing in. A labyrinth of slum alleys – ending in a dead end. Every undead, every monstrosity, and every slaughter was just a joke to send us down another wrong path. The Necrolord did not care about throwing her undead servants at us. She cared even less about the gangsters. And never was the resistance from the undead and the gangsters ever apparently necessary. We uncovered countless flesh factories and warehouses full of stolen organs and corpses. You'd think that meant we were making progress. We were not. Every flesh factory destroyed was replaced by two, if not three, more.

James Montague was balding from stress. Drake was smoking a full box of cigarettes every time I saw him.

I dedicated most of my time to the mission, tallying up days of missed classes, lectures and assignments. I could make up for them. The crusade was more important. Trying to stop the slaughter and bring my nemesis to justice was more important. What I did not shirk, however, was time with Colin. When I wasn't working, sleeping or having the rare time on campus, I spent time in Colin's arms.

We still hadn't had sex, but I was enjoying myself. Enjoying myself when I wasn't thinking more deeply about my predicament, that is. About how I wanted both Colin and the crusade. Could I really reconcile the duality of my life? Could I have love while still walking down my dark path? But there were times of happiness inbetween my brooding. I had not been intimate with anyone in high school or during my time at university. I was making up for it with Colin. A lot. That didn't mean that Colin and I still didn't talk. We talked about all manner of things. While we had allowed an open tenderness and romance into our relationship, we were still foremost friends. And I wouldn't have it any other way.

I arrived home, sweaty and covered in the blood of zombies, when I got the usual urge to phone Colin to see if he could come over or if I could go over there.

"Hey," I said. I considered calling him something silly like 'babe' or 'sweetie', but that seemed unnatural. "Just got home from a hunt. Wanting to unwind. Stream and chill at my place?"

"Hey, Kat," he said, with genuine warmth. "Would love to but can't. Pranish has me running ragged. We're closing off on the final contract insertions and he's got me chanting so much lawmantic script that I'm considering becoming an anarchist and renouncing my love of authority."

"Let's hope he works you harder, then! Authority is overrated."

He laughed, and we talked a bit more. I was disappointed that he couldn't come over but it wasn't too bad. Could probably try get some work done (as if!).

I heard Pranish call him and he said his goodbyes, making some overexaggerated kissy noises over the phone, which I laughed at and then hung up.

I was just about to put my phone away when it rang again.

"Don't answer it," Treth said, he sounded worried. He must've seen the caller ID already.

"Why?" I asked, then I realised why.

Andy.

"Why'd he be calling?"

"Who you talking to?" Duer asked.

"Treth."

"Oh, to yourself. Never mind."

I rolled my eyes. Duer still didn't believe me about Treth.

The phone kept ringing. What would that asshole want?

"Don't answer it," Treth repeated. "He's a waste of time."

"You used to like him," I said.

"So, did you. We both got over that. Look at us learning, together."

I frowned at the phone. It stopped ringing. And then started ringing again.

"It could be something important."

I felt the sting of apprehension.

"It could be about Trudie. Something might have happened."

I pressed to receive the call but didn't speak.

"Kat…" I heard Andy speak. It was slurred. Was he drunk?

I didn't answer.

"I hear you, Kat," he said. "I hear you…breathing…"

He slurred heavily between words, and his tone was angry. My rational brain told me to hang up. My curious Kat (see what I did there?) brain told me to keep listening.

"Why won't you talk to me?!" he suddenly yelled.

Probably because you're yelling, I would have said if I didn't want to give him the satisfaction of a reply.

"I'm sorry that I didn't help!" he yelled again. "I really…um…am. But…"

He restrained a burp, or a hiccup, or both.

"I need you," he said, quieter. "I love you."

That caught me by surprise. If I wasn't speechless before, I really was now.

"I loved you since I laid eyes on you, Kat. I knew I needed you. So strong. So…beautiful. That prat doesn't deserve you."

He was shouting again.

"I deserve you! What happened? Why won't you talk to me?"

I let the silence lengthen. I really knew I should've hung up. To stop humouring him. To deny him with dial tone, but I stayed on.

"Why won't you love me?" he whispered. "Please tell me. I'll do anything."

The silence drew on, and I felt my anger rise.

How fucking dare he! He was dating my best friend and had the sheer audacity to pull a stunt like this!

"Just fuck off," I said, coldly. Like I was on a hunt. I hung up.

I can keep a cool head, most of the time. But not now. He had betrayed me before, and now he'd betrayed Trudie twice.

I threw my phone across the room onto the couch. My anger abated too fast, however, and I found my head swimming. I staggered and caught myself on the wall.

"Are you okay?" Treth asked, the genuine concern in his voice letting me find my balance. I liked to hear his voice. It reassured me.

"Yeah, yeah. Just…wasn't expecting that."

"I told you not to pick up."

"You knew he'd do something like that?"

"I suspected it. That guy is…not right."

"Tell me about it."

"What are you gonna do?"

I pondered the thought, and my speeding heart.

I faced monsters for a living. I slay horrors for petty cash. But that unnerved me.

"I'll talk to Pranish first. See what he thinks."

I went to retrieve my cell, despite it still feeling dirty after Andy's call, and then called Pranish.

"Busy, Kat," Pranish said.

"Is Colin there?"

"No. Next room. You talked to him a few minutes ago. Lay off."

His tone belied his humour. He was suffering from PTSD and was overly focused on his work, but he was still my humorous friend at his core.

"I need to talk to you…"

How was I going to put this?

"Just don't tell Colin. I don't think he'd take it well. Might do something stupid. I just got a call from Andy."

"Don't tell me you're wanting to get…"

"Don't you dare finish that sentence. The prick called me while drunk then started yelling at me. Railed off about being in love with me. Was creepy as fuck."

I was speaking fast. Very fast.

"Woah-woah, slow down, Kat."

I started to repeat myself.

"Nah, I got all it. Just struggling to believe it…"

I was silent as he processed the information.

"You sure it was him?" he continued.

"Who else could it be? I'm not that popular."

"Definitely not…"

I could practically hear Pranish's mental gears turning.

"Trudie needs to know…" he said. "But she won't believe you. She's convinced you like Andy and this is some sort of twisted dating game."

"She's being stupid."

"Yeah, obviously, but she's still our friend."

I didn't disagree.

"Anyway," he continued. "Be alert. Download a call recording app. If he calls again, switch it on and record what he says. We can play it to Trudie. She won't believe we'd go through the effort to fabricate something like that."

I nodded, then realised I was on the phone, and said, "Thanks, Pranish."

"No need. Let's sort this out. For Trudie and…"

He was about to say himself but stopped.

"Anyway," he said. "Need to get back to work. Colin, you've got those scrolls primed? Excellent."

He hung up.

I stared at the phone screen for a few moments, and then slumped down on the couch.

"It'll work out," Treth said. "You've got Colin and Pranish by your side. And Trudie will come around eventually."

"I know, I know. Just…wasn't expecting it at all. Creeped me out more than the Necrolord."

"Foolish. The Necrolord is a lot more terrifying."

"You think so?" I agreed with him, of course, but just wanted to encourage him to speak. I didn't want to be left in silence.

"A monster in the light is an easy target. We have never seen the Necrolord outside of the dark. She's elusive. Like…"

"The unrelenting darkness two weeks back. And the moving shadows in that stronghold yesterday…"

"Exactly."

I sighed. For now, thoughts of Andy were at the back of my mind. The Necrolord regained the forefront.

"What is her goal?" I asked.

"If we knew that, she'd be easier to catch. You catch an animal by putting out something it desires. Bait. We find what she wants, we find a way to draw her out."

"Doesn't help us," I said, resigned. "We know so little about her. I don't like it. I'm used to fighting undead I understand. Even Jeremiah, Cornelius and Digby were easier to decipher than this. All we know is that she likes me, for some reason, and sugared cereal."

"Could be something there we could use."

"Could be, but not now. I call for a time-out."

"Right-o. I dare say you've earned it."

"Hah, haven't been too bad yourself, Treth. Thanks for that call-out earlier, by the way. Almost lost my head."

"Anytime."

I proceeded to have a nice, hot shower, followed by a dinner of a double portion of instant noodles (chilli flavoured). After that, I contemplated studying and then decided I was too tired for that (let's say I've lost my zest for academia). I watched some videos on *YouTube* and by

155

the time I dredged up the willpower to pull myself away from funny cat videos, it was very late. I brushed my teeth and went to my bedroom, carrying a copy of *The Law* by Bastiat. Colin wanted me to read it. He was excited about it, so I couldn't say no.

Just as I was about to close my bedroom door behind me, Duer whimpered.

"Kat…"

I immediately remembered an image of a white demon clinging to my window and shivered. But the lights were still on. No voidcreeps. No demons.

"What is it, Duer?" I whispered.

"Blood," he said. "Blood on the window."

I turned on my lounge light, and as Duer had said, there it was. Blood was coating my window, forming chilling letters.

"It looks like…" Treth said. "An address."

"And a time," I added. "Tomorrow night. It seems that the Necrolord wants to meet."

"Will we go?"

"Do we have a choice?"

"No."

I nodded, punctuating the point, and then turned back into my bedroom to sleep.

Chapter 12.   What   goes around…

The morning air was cool on my skin as I leaned up against the wall of Colin's apartment complex, *The Law* in my hands. It was early. An hour before class. The birds singing could still be heard over the mounting traffic. I hardly slept last night. Don't get me wrong. I wasn't scared. I'd witnessed much harsher things than a blood-stained window. But it had spurred an anticipation in me.

The Necrolord wanted to meet. After all this time. What was I supposed to think about that? And what would it involve? It was obviously some sort of trap. But the message had just been an address and time. Tonight. A warehouse in North Road. Fitting, as North Road was where I'd met the Necrolord for the first time. Now, that was a memory that brought shivers. The Necrolord had infused me with coal-like blood, escaping as I thought I was choking. A petite figure, wearing a black hoodie.

Was the Necrolord a child?

I banished the thought. No child held such intense malice, nor had the experience. The will.

You did.

That wasn't Treth who spoke. It was me. And I couldn't disagree. Treth didn't know about my dark times after my parents died. Only I did. And only I knew what I had been willing, was still willing, to do to avenge them.

"Kat?" Colin greeted, with a hint of confusion in his voice as he yawned, about to leave for court. He was dressed up in his business suit, looking all cute. Like a penguin. A small part of me felt embarrassed at the thought. The other part didn't care. Colin was my boyfriend. I could think what I wanted.

"Hey, Colin," I said. His eyes drifted down to the book in my hands.

"Enjoying it?" Was that a flicker of both worry and excited anticipation in his eye?

I looked down at the page. I'd forgotten I was holding it. But I had absorbed some of it.

"I am, actually. The religious aspect is a bit unnecessary, but…yeah."

He approached more closely, the unmistakable hint of worry creasing his brow. I felt his warmth, even at this distance, and wanted him closer. Damn class and damn court for stopping us!

"What's up, Kat? Something happen?"

Too much. Andy. The Necrolord. Blood, blood, and more blood. And everything that had come before. Some day, I'd need to tell him. And hopefully, he would still love me afterwards.

"I have a mission tonight," I said. "It may be dangerous."

I bit my lip. He didn't say anything.

"I'll have people I trust with me, so it should be fine, but…"

"I know, Kat." He tried to smile. I hugged him, burying my head in his shoulder so he couldn't see the moisture in my eyes and that I couldn't see his.

"I'll see you after…if you'd like."

"I would."

"Even if its 3am?"

"When else would we see each other? During the day? Like normal people? Hah!"

I laughed. And it felt good. I released him and he me. The tears were not going to come any more. We saw each other off. And I rode away.

***

160

In many ways, I am lucky to have Treth. Before a battle, and before possible death, most people have to face an intense silence. A quiet contemplation that would drive lesser men to madness. I had a ghostly voice inside my head. I was already mad.

In between classes, I had phoned Montague. He agreed with me that it sounded like a trap, but we had to pursue every lead we could. He also agreed with me that we didn't want to scare the Necrolord away just in case it wasn't a trap. So, we had to compromise between safety and prudence. I handpicked Brett, Guy and a few other hunters to be my guard. Whiteshield and Puretide squads were to be stationed a few streets over. The second they heard gunshots, they'd rush in. I just hoped that they'd be fast enough if things really got bad.

Bringing Brett and Guy was a no-brainer. I trusted them over any other hunter. For the others, I relied on Brett's recruiting. But there was one other guy I chose. Hammond, the Puretide sorcerer, who'd been aggro with me before I saved his life by cutting off his arm. He only needed the one arm to be an adept spellcaster. And after that entire affair, he felt he owed me. So, I brought him along. Could always use more sorcerers.

It wasn't time for the mission yet. A few hours to go. The others would be alone, with their quiet musing. Even if they had company, they'd be alone. This wasn't going to be like the other missions. This time, we were invited. And that was more terrifying than any no-knock-raid.

Unlike the others, I was never really alone. Treth was always with me, and while we were not privy to each other's thoughts, he did not give me the silence needed for brooding. I was thankful for that.

"Weapons checked?" he said. He knew I had checked them. We'd done it together, obviously. It was a mental check for both of us.

I hummed my assent.

"Coat still hot?"

"Always."

"Why do you keep talking to yourself?" Duer piped in.

"Because nobody else is worthy enough of a conversation partner," I replied. He looked a tad offended and then flew over to his flowerbed to pout.

I sat down. There was no point standing in my own apartment for this mission. I could try relaxing a bit.

"How about you?" Treth asked. "You ready?"

I started a nod but stopped. I sighed.

"It used to be simpler."

"It used to just be a few rotting zombies and an old lady who couldn't pay the going-rates," Treth said.

"Not just that…it used to be simpler to just go in…"

"But now you have something to lose."

I bit my lip. I felt Treth's presence grow, as if he was sitting beside me, putting his arm around my shoulders to comfort me in my reverie.

"We'll get through this. We always do. And Colin will be waiting for you when we're done."

I couldn't help but smile, just a bit.

"You're definitely a Team Colin guy, aren't you?"

"There's teams?"

"Team Brett. Not saying I like him that way, but you obviously really don't want me to."

"Brett is…" Treth's tone changed to something much more contemplative. "He's a good fighter."

"Whoa, tone down the flattery," I joked. "Else I'd think you were into him."

Treth snorted. "Brett is fine. But not for you. A hunter shouldn't date another hunter."

"Why?"

"Who comes home to whom?"

"They come home for each other. Together."

"But when the one dies…"

"A hunter accepts death, Treth. They accept the loss. They go back to the hunt."

"And come home for?"

Nobody.

Was the unvoiced reply.

I looked at the watch that Colin gave me.

"It's about time. Let's go."

***

The warehouse was barely lit by a single yellow-tinted light-bulb over a door next to the larger entrance. I couldn't help but feel a bit uneasy. I'd been in a lot of warehouses throughout my career. They seldom contained anything pleasant. But I'd come out of each alive. This would be the same. It had to be.

Brett and Guy took point. Hammond was by my side. He'd recovered soon after being bitten by the zombie, and my subsequent amputation. Hadn't given me any lip after that. In fact, he stood next to me like a loyal golden retriever. He was stretching his fingers on his remaining arm, ready to cast. Hopefully, we wouldn't need to.

Brett looked at me, his eyes still visible through his now full gas-mask. The fear around the miasma had caused Drakenbane and Puretide to go all out on magical respiratory systems. His eyes were questioning. He wanted to know if I was sure about going in. This was a trap. We all knew it. But everything else had also been a trap.

I nodded, and he opened the door. We entered, passed boxes and then into the open.

The warehouse was dark inside, except for a single bright spot in the centre. At its periphery, stood a tall woman, clothed in black leathers. She had red hair. Long. Down to the small of her back, at least.

"You're not the Necrolord," I said, simply. I said it instinctively, as if I'd know what the Necrolord would look like.

"Very astute, Drummond," the woman replied, barely hiding the venom in her voice. She was angry. Very angry.

"Do you serve her?" I asked. "I didn't expect vampires to work for the Necrolord. But it seems anything is possible."

The woman walked forward, confirming my suspicions. She had red eyes, skin as pale as printing paper, and I saw the hint of fangs when she opened her mouth.

"This isn't about the Necrolord, Drummond." She said my name again, as if it was a curse.

"Well, then we've got a problem," I said, my left-hand drifting behind my back, where Voidshot was holstered. Silver wouldn't kill a vampire outright, but it would stop it from regenerating at the point of impact. "You see, we're being paid to hunt a necromancer. You're currently sapping up tax payer's money with this false call out. That's a criminal offence."

"And what you did wasn't?" she shouted.

The shout shocked me, but not as much as the others. Brett levelled his shotgun right at the creature, and I heard clicks as Guy aimed both his machine-pistols, flicking off the safeties. I had almost forgotten their background with vampires. It wasn't pretty. And this wasn't going to remain pretty. But I kept on talking. Needed to find out everything I could.

"What are you talking about?"

She came closer, but still far enough away that we didn't fire. I could see the bags under her eyes. Sleepless days, yet vampires didn't need to sleep.

"Do you know about the connection between a sire and her ward?"

"You mean leach and its victim?"

"You know nothing, sun-drinker! What we give is a gift. A gift that connects us to each other. Connects everything! Even across the In Between..."

She was tensing her fists, but I could still see her claws. Like steel nails protruding from her fingertips. She was an advanced vampire. Already had mutations. This wasn't going to be pretty. I backed away, just slightly.

"I felt everything you did to him," she whispered. "I felt, and heard, his screaming as you scorched him. And then later, I felt the bite of your steel on his flesh. I felt him even as his head hit the ground. And until the end, he was thinking about me."

Oh, Athena...I remembered. Henrik. The vampire that I had tortured to save Trudie. I'd held him under the sun, and then executed him when he gave away our position. But this she-vamp didn't have the Blood Cartel's under-eye tattoo. She wasn't Blood Cartel. But tattoos could be removed, or vampire politics could be as complex as human politics.

"Kat, get behind us," Brett whispered, his voice steely. Cold. It was the least human he'd ever sounded. Was this the Extermination Corps coming through?

"I let you bring your friends for a reason," the lady-vamp continued. "I knew you'd bring your accomplices. And even now I remember Henrik's memory of them. Their voices. Now, I don't have to track you all down. He'll be avenged. And you'll all die for taking him away from me."

It all happened at once. One of Brett's Drakenbane buddies cried out from behind us, the she-vamp rushed forward in a black and white blur, and Hammond rushed in front of me, releasing a wall of flame that almost baked me like brownies. But it provided me with the delay I needed. I drew Voidshot and my wakizashi and fired through the flames. No cries heralded that I hit anything. I slashed out and caught something in the shadows. Another vampire, clothed in black, who had blended into the darkness with some of its vampiric treachery. My sword lodged in the side of the vamp's chest, biting into his lungs. He stared at me, grinning his fanged grin. I shot him right in the face. He wasn't grinning anymore. But didn't mean he was dead. Vampires were complicated that way.

Before I could find my bearings, she was on me, slashing with her hand-claws. Thank Trudie for my hardened wakizashi! Only magic could withstand such blows, as I parried the she-vamp's berserk onslaught with my sword, trying to back away into the melee. Gunshots deafened me, and Hammond (despite missing an arm) was sending out volleys of flames. I couldn't see Brett. Hells, I couldn't see anything but the monstrous woman before me, and the sparks flying off my blade and her claws.

"We never forget those who hurt us," she said, not stuttering or even break a sweat as she raked every-which-way. It was a miracle I managed to keep my blade up. And as miracles often do, it stopped, and I felt the acidic bite of her claws on my arm and shoulder. I gritted my teeth, but I wanted to cry out.

"You feel it, sun-drinker? You feel an inkling of the pain he felt? That I felt?"

She pulled her claws back and I slashed out at the opening, creating a wide gash over her breasts. She didn't flutter an eyelid. She slashed at me, and even as Brett

169

tackled me to the floor, I felt the rush of air bite through my armour.

My respite, winded and bleeding on the floor with Brett on top of me, gave me time to see how many of my men had died. My men. Why the hell did I only think of them now that they were dead? We love to find ways to hurt ourselves, don't we? Not enough that they're dead. Now I must suddenly feel responsible for them.

Brett rolled off me and fired his shotgun, pumped, and then the barrel was sliced off. No hardening enchantment. He ducked under another slash and pulled out a bowie knife from an ankle-sheath. I stood up, feeling the blood dripping down my arm with ever-increasing speed. Red coated my gloves, shirt and the hilt of my blade.

The she-vamp only had me in her sights, as she turned from Brett, and charged at me, her face ablaze with fury. She cried out as Brett struck her in her Achilles' tendon. Must've been silver. Only silver could cause a vamp pain and stop their regeneration around the wound.

With her slowed, I fired at her with Voidshot, using my silver rounds. She grunted with every impact, a blackened hole appearing on her milky flesh. But she pressed on, dragging Brett with her as he tried to keep her pinned.

My coat flared as a vampire tried to attack from behind. At least they were still human enough to fear fire.

"Kat!" Hammond shouted. I looked at him and he muttered some words. My blade shone a splendid orange-gold and I felt its hum of power. My sword wasn't silver, but this would do.

"Henrik was a monster," I shouted at the she-vamp. She roared in response. Brett's face was red with the strain of holding the beast still. That's why I needed to taunt her, so she wouldn't turn on him.

I fired at her again, planting a sizzling hole in her head. She staggered, but looked back at me, eyes white. Like a zombie.

"And so are you…"

I holstered Voidshot and held my wakizashi with two hands. I held my breath, and charged, releasing my blade with a brutal underarm swing that met flesh, bone, and cleared it. Brett let go of the she-vamp's legs, letting them fall as the top half of her torso went flying, landing in the hand of one of her henchmen. He was missing an arm and had shotgun holes all over his chest.

"We never forget, Drummond," half the she-vamp shouted. "We're coming for you!"

Brett fired at the vampires with his pistol, but they were already gone, blending into the shadows. Hammond shot out a wall of flame, but there was nothing left.

Just us and the warehouse, surrounded by our dead. I didn't see a dead vampire among them.

"We should've brought silver," Brett muttered.

"We couldn't have known," Guy replied.

"Then we've gotten soft. They're always at the edge of the shadows. Always!"

Guy nodded, sternly.

I still stared at the space where they'd disappeared, until I couldn't handle it anymore, and I collapsed to my knees.

I'd almost died tonight.

Chapter 13.   Comes around

I'd been wounded before. Much worse than this. I'd brushed up so closely to death that I'd thought it was my friend. I'd lost part of my scalp to a wraith, had myself eviscerated, been shot-gunned by bone-matter and crushed by an archdemon. Why then did this feel so much worse? Perhaps, because this wasn't a monster I'd been paid to fight. And that I'd been the one to kick the hornet's nest.

I thought my attack on the Blood Cartel had been forgotten. Even the vampire lobbyist had stopped the search for the four vampire murderers who'd shot up the Quantum bar. That's what we'd thought, at least.

We were wrong.

The back-up squads had all been wiped out. They hadn't expected vampires. Like Brett had said, they hadn't had silver. And they had not expected the shadows to engulf them and tear them apart. The only survivor was barely that, as his shallow breathing, fang marks and greying skin revealed his oncoming ghoulification. Brett put him down. His eyes were hollow, yet angry. And I could see his training then. His role in the Extermination Corps. He hated vampires. More than I even hated the undead. I understood a bit of why Treth was afraid of my affection for him. Brett was broken, even more so than I was, and broken people like us needed a fixer, not each other.

And my fixer was Colin, and that is why I stood outside his apartment block, at 2am, my bandages still leaking red even after healing spells and poultices.

Colin came rushing down before I could call him or press the doorbell. He embraced me, and my coat didn't attempt to incinerate him.

"I saw the glow of the coat from inside," he said. "I couldn't sleep."

"I'm sorry," I said, my voice still and unemotional. But then tears rushed to my eyes, as his warmth pressed up against me. I'd almost lost this. Too many times. I collapsed in his arms.

"I'm sorry!" I croaked out again, sobbing. And repeated it, again and again, even as Colin tried to console me.

I didn't remember entering Colin's home, and I was only awoken from my reverie by the smell of tea and the feel as Colin wiped away my tears. He put his arm around me and I heard the faint hiss as one of his tears fell on my flaming coat.

I spent the night with Colin. In his arms, with him comforting me, being my fixer. Eventually, my tears stopped, and in his arms, darkness embraced me, and I slept.

***

We didn't do anything in the night. Neither of us wished to do anything else but be near each other as I scraped past death once again. I didn't tell him what happened in the warehouse. I didn't need to.

In the morning, Colin made me bacon and eggs. Much more substantial than my usual fare of ramen 24/7. Pranish hadn't been there the night before. Colin said he was at a family thing. Knowing Pranish's family, I really hoped for my friend's sanity. He was an adept wizard, but a weakling in the eyes of his sorcerer family. I really wasn't a fan of Pranish's siblings or parents.

While Colin was washing up, I received a text message. Brett.

"Silver plated axes." It read, with a link to the website to buy them. "We'll be ready next time."

175

"He never stops," Treth said.

"Neither do we," I whispered.

I sheathed my cell as Colin re-entered, taking his seat opposite me and touching my hand.

"I want you to move in," he said. Well, wasn't expecting that. Before I could reply, he continued.

"I can't help you on your missions, but I want to be able to help you, some of the time. To make sure you're safe."

"Colin…"

"I understand if it is too much…" he raised his hands diplomatically. "Too soon, and…all that."

"It's not that…it's just…" Well, it was that. I like Colin. I really do. But I live by myself for a reason. I like my own space. I looked around at the large apartment. Colin had told me that he lived alone, funded by a well-paying job and money from his parents who owned a farm near North Guard.

Did I want to move in with him? Could I? Funnily enough, I liked my shoe-box apartment. And would Duer and Alex handle me moving out? I don't think they would.

"I don't want to move in," I said, but before Colin registered his own dismay. "But if you'd like, you can move in with me. If just for a bit. Until this is all over."

He nodded and smiled faintly. We spent the rest of the morning in silence.

***

"They're doing what?!" I asked a bit too loudly, drawing stares from other students on Jammie Plaza as I spoke to Conrad on the phone.

"That vampire is after you, Kat. Whiteshield specialises in human and vampire assailants. They're going to guard your apartment."

"I can handle myself."

"Not all the time. You have to sleep eventually. And vampires aren't like those voidcreeps. They don't need an invitation."

He paused, and I heard him take a sip of his coffee. I didn't respond. I was fuming. How could I live with Whiteshield stationed around my apartment? I'd just accepted that I should let Colin stay over and occupy my precious private space. Now I was going to need to navigate around smug, brutish mercenaries. All because some vampire bitch decided she wanted me dead.

"Any information on the vampires?" I finally asked, through gritted teeth. I would return to the Whiteshield issue another time.

"Charlene Terhoff. Fugitive. Previously aligned with the Sanguineas syndicate. Not your problem anymore."

"Sounds like it still is."

"Especially if she wants your head," Treth added.

I nodded, affirming Treth's reply, but remembered that Conrad couldn't hear him.

"She wants me dead, and guards are an inconvenience. We need to get her out of the way."

Out of the way? I was sounding colder and colder every day. Sure, she was a vampire. A monster. But I had killed her…lover, I presume. Did I feel guilty? No…yes…a bit. But no time for that. A hunter doesn't cry over every death they cause. They just lose more and more sleep.

Conrad sounded hesitant. "Not that simple, Kat. The cops were very insistent that you focus on the Necrolord case."

"Can't I do both?"

"Apparently not."

"Ah, such faith in me!"

Conrad snorted, amused. "Anyway, watch your back, and don't slice up the Whiteshield guys when they're at your place."

He hung up. I kept the phone to my ear, so I could speak to Treth without looking mad.

"There's something weird going on with this case."

"Why do you say that?"

"Whiteshield guards? I'm not a national key point or Council VIP. I'm a private freelancer. Whiteshield gets called out to guard the Titan Magi, not some UCT student."

"Complaining that they value you?"

"Pfft, politicians don't value anything but themselves…"

"They value their tools."

"Which means I'm a tool," I answered, a hint of irritation coming through. I didn't like being used. There was a reason I was self-employed.

"A tool to beget the end of the Necrolord. I see no problem," Treth replied, in the voice he used for issuing platitudes. "A hammer does not resent being used to hit nails, for that is its function."

"And my function is?"

"To kill monsters."

"But that's just it, isn't it? I was already killing monsters. No real change, except that I'm being kept on a shorter leash. Tell me, Treth, does the hammer resent its user if it could undertake its function better alone?"

"A hammer doesn't truly resent anything, Kat. It's a hammer."

"You came up with that metaphor. Don't take it literally."

There was a pause, and Treth replied in a much more sombre tone.

"I didn't want to put any more worries into your head, and didn't want to ruin your time with Colin, but I have been worried about some stuff."

I narrowed my eyes, glaring. A first-year walked within my gaze, took one look at me, and then scampered away as fast as she could.

"What kind of stuff?"

"I'm sure you have also thought about it. The Council has never been this riled. Ever. It's not like this is the biggest crisis to hit Hope City. Remember the Scouring of North Guard from class?"

I did. Happened over 30 years ago. Orc raiders from the Northern Badlands entered the State of Good Hope and annihilated countless farms and settlements. They made it all the way up to Stellenbosch when the Zulu Empire agreed to a treaty to allow the Cape Defence Force to abandon their posts at the Three Point Line. The Empire were the enemies, but they still had some honour. And nobody liked orcs. Until the army got the treaty, however, the Council did nothing to stop the orcs. Only posted up a few bounties.

"This is different. These are undead…" I argued.

"And since when has the Council ever taken undead seriously?" Treth retorted.

Never. I didn't need to say it. The Council only put up miniscule bounties for the most threatening of undead. And necromancer warlords had existed in the slums since the late 90s. There was a reason I was struggling to churn a profit without Conrad. The undead didn't pay. Until now, for some reason.

"The Necrolord has the Council riled," Treth continued, his voice dripping with the tone of a conspirator. "The question is: what is different this time? Why this necromancer and not the others? Why not the vampires, why not the orcs, why not the hordes of zombies that came before? Why now and why her?"

I couldn't answer him. And I wouldn't need to. When I found out, Treth would. But by then, would it be too late?

Chapter 14.   Threats

Unlike the vampires, the Necrolord hadn't contacted me since her initial communications.

We continued to raid her strongholds, arresting and slaughtering her human gangsters, while purging the undead. We became numb to the horrors within her dark realm, but we didn't feel any closer to defeating her. And while I simultaneously wanted to understand everything about her in order to end her, I felt almost thankful that I did not. I did not think I could cope with knowing the inner workings of such a twisted mind.

Whiteshield had been suspicious of Colin as he moved in, but I gave them a piece of my mind. Mrs Ndlovu had not liked it one bit. She was just as much a fan of the government as I was, and while Whiteshield was technically a private contractor, it was basically an arm of the Council. I needed to make it up to her, somehow. Eventually. When this was all over. If it ever came to be over.

Throughout all the raids, routine slaying and frustration-filled debriefings, Treth's suspicions burrowed deeper and deeper into my mind. It had been over a month now. Well over. And the Council was still dedicated to this. And I could not come to believe that the reason was altruistic.

My suspicions brought me to the computer labs on campus between classes, where I dug through old archived newspapers, looking for any reason why the Council would react so harshly to this, and not anything else. Of course, I was greeted on the computer by three emails. A warning that I was going to fail history, another for undead studies, and another for vampiric lore.

I did not care.

The hunt, and the reasons behind it, were more important. I could repeat the year. But the Necrolord needed to be slain, and I needed to know why the Council was so interested in her.

I searched on the internet and through the archives for any lead I could think of. A comparable series of events, in particular. The closest events I could find were the assassination attempt of Chairman Dawi 15 years ago and the almost awakening of Adamastor just after the Cataclysm. These were, by no means, comparable to the rise of a necromantic warlord. The assassination attempt was on the chairman of the Council, so it was to be expected that they'd care about that. And the awakening of the Titan Under the Mountain was potentially world-ending, giving even the most apathetic bureaucrat cause for alarm. And while the Necrolord was responsible for mountains of dead in the slums and a few piles in Old Town, other monsters and mages had done worse with less of a reaction. I thought the abomination may have been the cause of this rage but, after it was dead, that should've been the end of it. No more attacks in Old Town after that. The Council didn't care about revenge. It cared about keeping the city from being crushed by the Titan or occupied by the ever-growing Empire to the east.

"The Council doesn't stay the same," Treth whispered, in his contemplative fashion. "People change. Intents change. Only the gods remain the same."

That may be something. I was thinking about this all wrong! The Council wasn't some cold, calculating hive-mind. It was made of up people. And people did care about revenge.

Was there a councillor with enough pull to redirect so many resources to a manhunt? Was it a personal vendetta? Or something colder?

And most importantly: who was responsible?

I made a list of councillors, with Zieg DuToit of Sanitation in red pen because I didn't like him. I also noted Henry Garce, Andy's father. He was the district councillor of Old Town. I divided them into groups based on their roles in the convoluted hierarchy of the Hope City Council. While the Chairman was meant to be a first-among-equals, I placed the current Chairman, Lucian Weston, at the top, with the councillors underneath criss-crossing based on their allegiances to a party, a ministry, or a district.

This revealed nothing. Well, what did I expect? I'm not a detective and undergrad history doesn't really teach that much investigative research.

I shook my head.

"It's hopeless. Feels like I'm just wasting time."

Treth grunted in response.

"I'm going home."

"You have a class."

"Don't feel like it."

"Remind me why you still insist on studying."

"I don't know. Habit, I guess."

I shut down the computer and left the IT lab, exiting the building to run into a familiar face.

"Hey, Kats," Oliver waved, even though he was just a few metres away from me. There was no one else around. It was afternoon and most people didn't use this exit. He was Andy's friend. I really didn't want to talk to him. I also really didn't like it that he was using Trudie's endearment for me.

I nodded my greeting but continued walking. He grabbed me by the arm, and I tensed up.

"Hey, hey. Just wanting to chat."

"About what?"

"This and that…"

My glare must've been one of my better ones, as he let go of my arm and avoided eye contact. Must say I was quite proud of that.

"I heard through the grapevine that Colin moved in with you," he continued, considering some dirt on the wall. While he averted his gaze, his tone remained unchanged.

"The grapevine must mind its own business," I countered, filling my voice with enough venom that it could poison a troll.

187

How did he know? It had only been a day ago that Colin had moved in. Was he, or someone else, watching me?

"Why you go for him, Kats?"

"Don't call me Kats."

It was quick, and subtle, but I noticed him bare his teeth, just a bit. Interesting.

"Andy's my friend. He likes you. And he met you before that twerp. You were unfair on him. More than unfair. You should really be dating him. He suits your…lifestyle much more."

"Doesn't seem like your call to make."

I turned on my heels, but he caught my arm. I felt his breath on my neck as he spoke into my ear.

"Andy's the one for you, Kats. And for Colin's sake, I hope you realise that."

The tone was unmistakably threatening. I didn't take kindly to threats.

I grabbed his arm, twisted it, and with my free hand, grabbed him by the throat like I would a lone zombie before execution.

"Don't you ever fucking threaten me or the people I love," I said.

"Love?" he snarled.

I ignored him.

"I kill monsters for a living, shithead. And I'm not unaccustomed to killing humans who piss me off."

He bared his teeth at me and I felt what seemed to be a silent vibration from his chest, but then it disappeared. He calmed, and I let go. He glared daggers at me, and then stalked away.

I watched him disappear into a campus building, and then I collapsed against a wall, panting.

"He's just a punk, Kat," Treth tried to calm me. "You handled it well."

"What if he's serious? What if they try to go after Colin?"

"Colin can defend himself. He's a man." I felt that Treth didn't truly believe his own words.

Before I could worry anymore, my phone rang. I checked the caller ID. Drake.

"What?" I answered.

"Hey, Kat," the private detective answered. "Something wrong?"

"Nothing," I lied. "What's up?"

"This and that. And it got me to thinking…" he was sounding his usual cocky self, but there was something off. A hint of hesitance in his voice. "How about I take you on a date?"

That last part was a shock and a half.

"I've got a boyfriend," I replied.

"That's not a problem," he said. "I'm sure I have something he doesn't."

There definitely wasn't something right with the way he was speaking. It sounded wooden. Insincere.

"Like what?" I answered, humouring him.

"A better trenchcoat, manliness, information befitting an investigator, and a license to carry a firearm."

There was something hidden there, and I noticed it. Information. Drake had something to tell me. Something he couldn't tell me over the phone.

"Where are you thinking of hosting this *date*?"

"The race tracks. By Killarney. Decent race tonight. 7pm"

I almost said that I had no interest in racing but remembered that this wasn't really a date.

"I'll see you there."

"Cheers." He hung up. Smooth.

"So," I said to Treth. "The plot thickens."

Chapter 15.   Carrying

I have to make a confession. I have scant respect for the law. And when someone close to me may be in danger, there's little I won't do to keep them safe.

Buying an illegal gun is easy in Hope City. Brett had a load of them. Didn't ask questions. Guns disappeared from firefight scenes all the time. Anyone who found them at another scene would find that their serial number (if they still had one) was linked to a now very dead owner.

I acquired a 9mm pistol from Brett and secreted it in a shoebox with some ammunition. I carried this to my apartment where I greeted my Whiteshield guards with a nod. They didn't even nod back. Damn robots. At least Puretide and Drakenbane agents had some personality, even if it was petulance and snark most of the time.

Colin was home, but had evidently just arrived, as he placed his blazer over the back of a chair.

"Hey, Kat." He smiled, causing a pang. "How was your day?"

I didn't need to voice my concerns. He noticed them immediately.

He hugged me, and asked, "What's up?"

"Some punks…"

"Punks? Human?" he almost laughed. "If you sent them to the hospital, it's their own fault."

I smiled, faintly. "Not like that, but I wish I'd sent them to the hospital. They haven't done anything to me…except."

This was the hard part. I chose to rip the band-aid off quick.

"It's Andy and his pissant friend, Oliver. They're threatening to do something to you."

"Me?" he asked, incredulous. "Why?"

"Because that fucker Andy thinks he owns me, for some reason."

Colin looked me in the eyes, trying his utmost to guess what I was feeling. I wondered what he saw.

"They won't do anything," he said. "They're punks. And if they did do something, I'd sort them out in Court so fast that we could go for a half-year vacation to Mauritius, paid for by their trust funds."

I tried to smile, but I couldn't.

"I don't think they'd give you the chance," I said.

Colin's smile wavered, just a bit. He may be an attorney, with a steely façade, but I could see through him. This worried him, too.

"They want me to leave you," I said.

"Will you?"

"Don't ask dumb questions."

I hugged him this time and squeezed.

"I'm still worried that they're gonna do something," I said, quietly, nestled into his shoulder.

"I can handle myself," he said, stroking my hair.

"I know, but…"

I let go of him and moved to the pistol in the shoebox. I'd placed it on the counter.

Colin managed to refrain from gasping.

"I'm not licensed!" he whispered, considering the Whiteshield guards just outside.

"As if that matters," I said, at speaking volume. What was anyone going to do with that statement?

Colin backed away from the firearm.

"What do you think I'm going to do with this?"

"Carry it. When you can. Just in case."

"You're…" he shook his head. "You're asking me to commit a crime. I'm a lawyer."

"Some laws are dumb. You have the right to defend yourself."

"I can't believe this." He shook his head.

"It's just a gun," I whispered. Did I do the right thing? Was I too hasty? Treth hadn't stopped me. But why would he? He was just as ignorant about these sorts of things as I was.

"It's an *illegal* gun. Pretty big detail. My responsibility is to the law. I might not be a cop, but the law still means something."

I moved towards him until our faces were just a hand-span apart.

"I face death every day," I whispered. "And the reason I come back has nothing to do with the law. I come back because I do what it takes to survive. Illegal. Legal. Moral. Immoral. Doesn't matter. I survive because I do what I have to do. And I won't let you die because of something as petty as the law."

I saw him about to argue, but then he looked down. He looked the closest to that mousey boy I'd saved from street-mages so long ago. He backed away, averting his gaze. I couldn't let it end this way. Not now. Not Colin.

"I…I think I love you," I said. Colin looked shocked, and I even felt that Treth was stunned that I'd air my feelings.

"And while I might not know what that means yet, I know that it means I want you to be safe. I can't force you to take the gun, but I need to know that you'll be safe when I can't be there for you."

There was a tense silence, and then he laughed, quietly.

"Some boyfriend, I am. I'm meant to be the one protecting you."

"You do," I said, without hesitation. "And I protect you. Delegation. We do what we do best."

I smiled, and he smiled back.

"Now," I said, a naughty thought coming into my head. "I've got a date tonight, so I'd like to spend some time with you before then."

I ambushed him with a kiss before he could react and pushed him towards the couch where I straddled him. Between kisses and grunts, he gasped.

"What date?"

I laughed and didn't give him time to breathe until much later.

Chapter 16.   Racing

Killarney racetrack was a cacophony of shouting, booming announcers, advertisers and motor engines. Drake sent me a text telling me to see him in the stands. He gave me some directions, but it still took me quite a while to wade through the mosh-pit of racing fans. I didn't like the noise, but I handled it better than I would have a year ago. Being around gunfire as much as I had for the last few months would to that to you.

Eventually, I found Drake near the back, where I could still barely hear conversation over the zooming and screeching of tires.

"Glad you could make it," he yelled, until I was a bit closer. He pulled my ear close to his mouth and spoke just loud enough, so I could hear. "Turn off your phone."

I reached for my phone, but also felt for Voidshot and my knife, just in case. I trusted Drake but that trust only went so far.

I turned off my phone and dropped it into an aluminium bag that Drake offered. His was already in there.

"Now, let's go somewhere a bit quieter."

I followed him around a brick wall separating the stands from a hall to the bathroom. I could still hear the ruckus, but it was much less intense.

"So," I said, now that I could hear myself think. "What is this *date* about?"

"Is it that hard to think that a dashing young man like myself would not want to charm a beautiful lady?"

He laughed as I rolled my eyes, but then his expression straightened. Business-time.

"I've been looking into things, Kat," he said.

"I'd hope so. That's your job."

He ignored my jibe and continued.

"Council is my employer here but after the mimic and Blood Cartel, I still owe you."

I spoke as he lit a cigarette.

"What's with the secrecy? We're both working for the Council. Not like you're spying."

"Don't test me, Kat. You should well know that your disdain and mistrust of the government is common knowledge. Cops mutter about you anytime they get. James has even given up trying to keep them in line. Most he can hope for is that they won't push you into an unmarked grave."

Well, that wasn't a pleasant piece of information. Maybe having Whiteshield monitoring my apartment was important for more than just stopping vampire assassins. Should've been a tad more diplomatic with the ticks.

"And while we may both be working for the Council at the moment, that doesn't mean we always will be," he continued.

He took a puff. "I found something. Something I'm pretty sure they know but tried to keep hidden from us."

Now, he had me interested.

"Starts five years ago. A graveyard in Plumstead. A grave robbery. Typical Hope City stuff. Enough necromancers in this city to have annual conventions. But you know all about that already. The kicker about this case: only two corpses were dug up. A couple. The Evergreens. You know more than I do that a necromancer would be much less specific with their robberies."

"Not if the stolen corpses had anything particularly unique about them. Deformity. Relationship to the thief…"

Drake nodded, acknowledging my point. "It took some digging, but I found a news article from the same week as the robbery. A few days prior. Apparently, a family had been the victim of a necromantic ritual in their own home."

I got an involuntary chill down my spine. I repressed a remembered image, swallowed and took a breath.

"Yeah, like yours," Drake said, a hint of sympathy in his eyes. "The article didn't mention the name of the family, but it did mention two things. The child had survived, and that it happened in Plumstead. Seeing both of these pieces of information, I attempted to go into the archives to learn more about the Evergreens. To find some connection. But I hit a wall. There was a blank space in the archives where there should have been the Evergreen family. The only mention of Evergreen I could find was in the report of the grave robbery and the only connection I could make was to the necromantic ritual that killed them. After that, no mention of the Evergreens for years. Until, just about a year ago, when a C. Evergreen was hired as a freelance mage by the Department of Sanitation…"

A screech of tires and cheers interrupted Drake and he took the chance to take a long drag. He really carried off the noire vibe well. Trench-coat, cigarettes and all. If he practiced wizardry, one could name him after a German city. Or did I make that joke already?

"The details of C. Evergreen's employment are vague, as freelancer job descriptions for Council departments often are. Helps them get shunted when it is time for retrenchment. I tried to look through the archives for a C. Evergreen, but expectedly found nothing. A ghost. More than a ghost. Not so uncommon, though. Plenty of immigrants hired by the Council. They wouldn't be in the records. So, C. Evergreen's presence on the employment roster wasn't so abnormal, but this surname kept me coming back for more. Call it a hunch. I just knew that if I dug further, I'd find something more. I searched deeper, until I found a very recent document, detailing the termination of C. Evergreen's employment. Contract ended three months early. It was dated on the same day that you were poking your nose around the Eternity Lounge after the Blood Cartel had taken your friend."

"The Eternity Lounge?" Just saying it made me put the pieces together. I'd found residue of miasma there. The same miasma the Necrolord used.

"The Necrolord was the one who helped the Blood Cartel with that abduction."

Drake smiled as he took another drag. "Bingo."

"So," I said, feeling like I was in a dream with all this information suddenly coming to me. "This C. Evergreen is the Necrolord."

"Perhaps. Regardless, they, or she, worked for the Council," Drake added.

"Which means they're hunting one of their ex-employees. Hiding dirty laundry?"

"Or eliminating a rogue agent."

"You watch a lot of spy thrillers?"

"I live a lot of spy thrillers." He grinned, but there was little humour behind it.

I sighed. "Doesn't change much. We still need to kill her."

"What it does mean is that the Council has been hiding info from us. And if they want her dead so badly, they should have given us everything on her."

"They don't want to embarrass themselves."

"They could have fed us manipulated info. The name, at least."

203

I shrugged. "You're the detective."

He nodded. "And you're the hunter. I hope that if they decide that we need to be terminated that you'll be able to come to my rescue."

I snorted. "Won't come to that."

"I hope so, Kat. I really do. But if my job has taught me anything, it is that when giants fight, the peasants get squished. And I'm feeling awfully peasantly at the moment."

Chapter 17.   Third Force

Drake's information didn't alleviate my concerns. With my suspicions that the Council was hiding something vindicated, I started to focus more and more on what they were doing rather than focusing on the killing of the Necrolord. All this accomplished was muddying the waters. It made my job harder, forcing me to play detective more and more. And it also made me experience the worst thing a hunter could experience: doubt.

Doubt leads to hesitation. Hesitation is death.

But how could I not doubt, after what Drake had revealed to me, and how it had led to me putting my own pieces of the puzzle together.

Having Colin living with me actually helped a lot. We still hadn't had sex, due to a combination of my anxiety and a total lack of energy from both of us as our deadlines drew nearer and nearer. Not like I cared about my academic deadlines, of course, but I felt that the Council was going to start demanding the Necrolord's head very soon, and that failure would lead to termination of the worst kind.

But could I slay the Necrolord now?

Sure, I'd killed a necromancer. I'd kill her like she'd killed so many before her. But I needed to speak to her first. To find out what the Council's role in this was. And if she revealed that the Council had abetted her crimes, I'd find a way to make them pay.

With all the walking corpses and necromancy over this investigation, I was honestly sick of my specialty cases. I needed something else to break the monotony. I'd even go for killing a drake! Even Treth was tired of hunting undead.

But picking a new case wasn't that simple. When I went on the MonsterSlayer App to check out the hunt listings, everything pertained to the Necrolord case. And I mean everything. Not a single nightkin, vampire, troll, goblin, drake…nothing. Just fucking undead.

What was going on?

I phoned Conrad.

"Hey, Kat," he said, with the most exhausted voice I'd ever heard him use. Concern for the App went to the side for now, as the well-being of my agent took precedence.

"Conrad? You sound like you haven't slept for a decade."

"I haven't," he joked, with no humour in his voice. "What's up?"

"The MonsterSlayer App. It has only undead cases. Nothing else. Not even a routine dire-rat extermination."

"Council took over the App," he replied, exhaustion almost overwhelming the distaste in his voice.

"How's that possible? Council isn't allowed to own enterprises. It's why the Titan Cult is private. Spirit of the Law is clear on that."

"Proxies. Whiteshield acquired it."

"Why?"

There was a pause. Conrad finally sighed.

"I'm tired, Kat. Very tired. I've been at this for far too long."

"How?" I repressed a laugh. "You don't look a day over forty."

"Thanks," he answered, sarcastically. "But I've been doing this for longer than anyone else, believe it or not. Since before Puretide and Drakenbane started stealing all my business. Since before Hope City was called Hope City."

"That old, huh?"

He ignored me. "I'm planning on retiring, Kat. After this case. And that's the reason I made sure you got it. After you get the Necrolord, you'll be set. No more petty hunts late at night. You'll have enough money and clout to start your own agency or join any of the others. You won't need me then, and then I can relax."

Conrad…retiring?

"Is this Conrad I'm speaking to, or a very well-trained mimic?" I tried to jest, but the joke came out flat. Conrad was leaving me. I didn't know that would upset me this much. He was so smarmy. Creepy. Tasteless.

But he was my friend. And he'd saved my skin.

I was going to miss him.

"Don't try to get me to stay," he said. "I've made up my mind. It's time I hang up my tie alongside my crossbow. I needed the money before, but now that's not relevant anymore."

The final sentence was dripping with a sad resignation that I never expected from my agent. What had happened to him?

I didn't want him to retire, but who was I to stop him?

"Thank you, Conrad. It's been a pleasure," I said, choking down a half-sob. Who would have thought? Me getting tearful over Conrad.

"Thank me when this case is over, Kat. Until then, it has been an honour."

I hung up.

"So, we're gonna be on our own?" Treth asked.

"No," I whispered. "Not alone. We've got friends now. More friends. Conrad helped us get here, but you heard him. He wanted me, us, to get to this point so we wouldn't need him any more."

Treth snorted. "Sounds like a cheap excuse for him to take a cut for your hard work."

"There's a lot you still have to learn about capitalism, my friend."

I rubbed my chin, thoughtfully.

"What is it?" Treth asked.

"Whiteshield owns the MonsterSlayer App now, ensuring that every hunter is paying attention to this case and this case only."

"Sounds like this conspiracy is bigger than we thought."

"We should check out a Whiteshield office," I said.

"To find what?"

"I don't know. Something. Something to find out how deep this goes."

***

Getting into the Whiteshield branch office was easy. I had a pass for all things pertaining to the Necrolord case, second only to James Montague. All I said was that I needed to look through their files to catch the necromancer, and the tired looking clerk let me right through to their archives – a tiny room lined with servers, filing cabinets and a single computer, glowing in the dark.

"This is worse than looking through the archives on campus," Treth whined.

I didn't reply. It was bad, but it had to be done. But I'd still have thought that Whiteshield would have some sort of organisation in their digital filing. Everything was just all over the place!

It took me a while to find anything useful, but I eventually came across the acquisition document. Conrad was right. Whiteshield now owned the MonsterSlayer App. The age of truly free market monster hunting in Hope City was at an end. But politics would come later. It seemed that something like this had happened before. Fifteen years ago. The MonsterSlayer App was temporarily suspended after 51% of its shares were bought by Whiteshield, and then sold to private investors afterwards. The dates of the acquisition lined up perfectly with the attempted assassination of Chairman Dawi.

I ran a search for Dawi and assassination and found newspaper clippings relevant to Whiteshield's interests. A treaty signing with the Southern Ogre Horde, incursions into the Eastern Cape, and a group of unlikely individuals who saved Dawi's life. The assassination attempt was pinned on the Goldfield Magocracy, but that was common knowledge. It was all stuff in the public eye, if a bit forgotten fifteen years later.

I couldn't help but frown while reading through these old newspaper articles. I had been five at the time. My parents had been alive. Was I happy then? I remember being happy. Even if I wasn't, a time before my parents died must have been better than this. Hunting the dead, investigating corrupt agencies, facing the darkness…

I shook my head, vigorously, to break myself out of my stupor. I felt Treth's concern, but he didn't press.

I dug deeper and found a contract of employment for Whiteshield to protect the Chairman during the assassination, but that wasn't anything new. Everyone knew that Whiteshield was the *de facto* security detail of the Chairman of the Council.

I'd read through a veritable mountain of records, and hadn't come closer to answering the crucial question: why did they need to buy-out the MonsterSlayer App during that time? And why now?

I scrolled through the documents again and again, not unveiling anything new, until Treth spoke.

"Isn't the date of this new acquisition a few months back?"

I checked again, and he was right. I'd skimmed right over that, assuming the buy-out was recent. It wasn't. Whiteshield had acquired the App months back, and kept it functioning properly until now. But that wasn't the biggest thing. They'd acquired the app around the same time that I was running my mimic case. Coincidence?

What had I been doing around that time besides the mimic? Answer was obvious: my run in with Blood Cartel. The vampire cult and gang had also been the power behind the mimic.

Out of curiosity, I ran a search for Blood Cartel, and found some documents. Reports on the recent attempt on my life, but curiously, reports on the Robben Island incident, where the Cartel tried to summon a dark vampiric god onto Earth.

Why would a private security agency specialising in fighting humans be concerned with vampiric gods and their cults?

Before I could ponder the thought any more, the door behind me opened. I was just able to close the document I was reading before I was spun around on the office chair to stare into the face of a buzz-cut drill instructor-looking brute of a man wearing the Whiteshield combat fatigues, and stripes denoting him as a sergeant.

"What the fuck are you doing here? Where's your fucking clearance?" he bellowed, looking me straight in my eyes. I was no longer proud of my own death-stare. If this man wasn't a drill instructor, he needed to become one. He'd melt the bravado of even the most troublesome recruit. In the past, I'd get through situations like this by acting tough. Well, not always acting. But here, my legs became jelly. Good thing I was sitting down. If I had been standing, I may very well have collapsed from fright.

How was I going to get out of this?

My phone rang at that moment, saving me. He glanced down at my pocket.

"You going to get that?"

"If I may."

He stood up straight and crossed his arms. I took that as assent. Seems he was all bluster. Maybe I did have clearance and he was just posturing.

Caller ID was unknown. I got a lot of these. Was either Trudie with a new phone, or the Necrolord wanting to talk smack. I answered.

"This is Drummond," I answered, keeping my eyes on the Whiteshield guy in front of me. His veins were bulging on his arms, but his eyes looked bored. Was this a game for him? Was he scaring me for fun and this interrupted him?

"Drake's dead," James replied, the sound of sirens in the background. I no longer looked at the Whiteshield sergeant. My vision almost blanked from the shock.

"What?!"

"In his house. Family dead too. Necromantic ritual. Come over here. Now!"

He hung up.

Drake. Dead.

The Whiteshield sergeant let me stagger past him without a word. I didn't pay him any notice. Drake was dead, and I couldn't help but feel that I was next.

Chapter 18.   Signs

Drake had asked me to protect him. I hadn't thought much of that at the time but, now that he was dead, it was the only thing I could think about. Drake had been a friend, of sorts. And he'd been relying on me. Some help that did him. And if I couldn't protect Drake, could I protect the other people in my life? Could I protect Colin? Pranish? Trudie? Myself?

Drake's house was surrounded by cop cars, their blue and red lights casting an eerie glow on the darkening street as the sun slowly set. Neighbours were muttering to themselves, spreading their own versions of the story. Some had seen a werewolf, some said it was a murder-suicide, others said it was a rift-surge. None of them knew what they were talking about. They were just making noise. Comforting noise to pretend that their neighbour hadn't just been chopped up, and that they were next. Stories, no matter their gruesome contents, are comforting. They help people pretend that life can be fiction, and that the bad things will never happen to them.

I approached the yellow police tape strung between patrol cars, surrounding Drake's suburban home. A cop, one I'd never seen before, blocked my way with his arm. He looked concerned.

"This is a crime scene, miss. And nobody with any sensibility should have to look at what's inside if they don't have to."

"Let her past, Vries," a cop sidled over. It was the smoker. From the bar. "This lady has no sensibility. She'll be just…fine."

Vries looked about to argue but, the look on my face must've made him change his mind. He let me past and I lifted the tape above my head.

"Are you sure you have to see this?" Treth asked, as I stood just outside of Drake's open door.

I nodded and crossed the threshold.

Drake was located on top of his dining room table. His arms and legs were nailed multiple times to the wood, with blood pooling at every entry point. A gaping chest wound was held open by pins, and his ribs had been snapped away, leaving his organs unprotected. I did not pay heed to his nakedness, but rather to his bruises, ritualistic cuts and the abject trauma on his face. There was blood spattering his body, like rain droplets. And it was still dripping. I looked up to see the bodies of a woman and girl, bolted to the ceiling, pale from the blood they had lost, and their stomachs cut open to slowly leak on top of their husband and father. They were paler than he was. Drake had watched them die.

I didn't vomit. I thought I would. The smell of puke nearby suggested that many people had already. Maybe the cop was right. Maybe I didn't have any sensibility. But I knew that to be wrong. I felt very strongly. But I didn't feel sick. I felt an unbridled rage at whomever had done this to my friend. And more than that, a rage at myself for not protecting him.

"It isn't your fault," Treth whispered to me. "Don't blame yourself. Never blame yourself. You couldn't have done anything."

I clenched my fists.

Couldn't have done anything.

Like a child. Impotent, restrained. Strapped down like an animal awaiting sacrifice. Watching her parents die. Grasping towards them. A little hand. Unable to do anything. Anything.

Anything.

"Kat," I heard, but all I saw were my parents before me, telling me to close my eyes. And the face of a man, impassive as he drove a dagger into my father's chest. Again. Again. Again.

And I couldn't do anything.

"Kat!" Treth yelled, and I was broken out of my violent reverie. I was still standing by the scene, my hands clenched. Nobody was looking at me. They were looking for prints, taking samples. Doing what cops do.

It was a calm scene. No one spoke a word. Yet, my heart threatened to burst out of my chest.

I shouldn't have come. Not to something like this. It was too familiar. Too similar. Too much of what happened to me. Did Drake witness what I did? And what did he feel as he watched his beloveds bleed out above him?

Failure.

And then he'd have died.

I took a step forward. A heavy, single step.

"Kat?" Treth asked, voice laden with concern that I didn't need. It was too late for concern. It wouldn't bring Drake back. Wouldn't unbreak me.

I took another step. And another. Until I was looking into Drake's terrified eyes and screaming maw. The pain in his eyes was not for his suffering. I could see that much. And I saw the stains of blood-streaked tears across his cheeks.

"I'm sorry…friend," I whispered, and closed his eyes and mouth, gently. Almost a caress.

Treth didn't try to tell me again that I wasn't to blame. He knew I wouldn't believe him. But I wouldn't wallow. I couldn't. I had more people to protect.

"Forensics says he died an hour ago, but the wounds are much older than that," James said, while he lit a cigarette and blew the smoke right into my face.

"Basic necromancy. Keeps the body barely alive. Keeps the soul trapped. Screaming," I replied, my voice sounding foreign to me. Did I really sound that clinical? That cold, while my friend lay dead?

"Neighbours don't report seeing anything credible. Just usual folk-tales. They didn't hear the screams. Didn't hear a struggle, even. We found two discharged shells from Drake's firearm, but the neighbours didn't hear gunshots."

"They'd have been at work," I said. "And sound-dampening magic is common."

James nodded, but his expression still looked angry. He walked closer and took his cigarette out of his mouth.

He looked me in the eyes, and I let him.

"We hired you because you're apparently the best," he whispered, harshly. "But now our head of investigation is dead. And for what? The Necrolord is still on the loose, hacking her way through every innocent she can get her hands on. Drake is dead, and we don't have any more leads. Nothing. All we have is you. And you seem more intent on playing games with Whiteshield and looking up recent history than finally ending this fucking case!"

I didn't break his gaze.

"I will avenge him," I said, simply, and then I turned away.

Treth only spoke as I neared my bike, out of earshot of onlookers and cops.

"We have to kill her, Kat. She's only going to get more powerful."

"Yes," I acknowledged. "But she didn't kill Drake."

"A necromancer did that ritual, Kat. A necromancer he was investigating. Who else would have killed him?"

I got on my bike but didn't start it. I watched the police perimeter. Every cop there. Which were genuine? Which were cowards? Which had helped kill my friend?

"There was no miasma in there, Treth. No sign of it at all. And the Necrolord has never dampened sound before."

"New tricks."

I shook my head. "And that ritual…she didn't do it. The Necrolord isn't like the old necromancers with their black cloaks, pomp and dark god sacrifices. She's practical. You've seen her operations. She keeps everything organised. Everything has its purpose…"

"Killing Drake seems practical…"

"Not like this. Not with his family in front of him. Not in a drawn-out ritual with so many fake ritualistic cuts that even a Puretide agent could see that the cuts were done by an amateur who'd only read about necromancy in old textbooks."

That shushed Treth. He was thinking now. Was looking past the horror. Analysing it. I felt his recognition. He realised it now, too.

"The Necrolord never cared who heard her, because she knew she could kill her opponents and be out of there before noise mattered. And why only kill Drake now?"

"Because…he was onto something?" Treth offered.

"Exactly. And we know what he found out. And it isn't the Necrolord who should be concerned about that information, but our employers."

I started the bike and drove away.

"What's our next move?" Treth asked, as the wind buffeted my clothes and we sped down tree-lined suburban streets.

"What I told James. I'll avenge Drake. If that means killing cops or Councillors as well as the Necrolord, so be it."

Chapter 19.   The Challenge

The Council sent me a formal letter telling me to get a move on. They used Drake as a tool to guilt me. To tell me that I was taking too long. The Necrolord had to be stopped, they said. Lest more cases like Drake happen again.

The veiled threat was clear, even if they didn't know it.

But the letter also smacked of desperation. Something was about to happen. Time was running out. For the Council, for the Necrolord, and for me.

Attacking strongholds and trying to brute force the Necrolord out of the slums hadn't been working. And it would never work. She was much too smart for that. The Council was trying to find a needle in a haystack by bombing the haystack. It wouldn't work. And I had to do something different to solve this case, before more people I cared about got hurt.

C. Evergreen. The name of the Necrolord. At least, the closest thing we had to a name. And by giving her a name, I couldn't help but see the Necrolord as human. And humans could be communicated with, even if I despised them.

Colin was at Pranish's. I noted that he had taken the gun, and that lifted a pressure off my chest. He wouldn't need to fire it. If Oliver and Andy tried anything stupid, a flash of it would send them running. I was sure of that.

Colin's absence did mean that I was alone, except for Duer and the Whiteshield guards posted outside. Alone with my thoughts, and Treth, who was also in one of his silences.

I knew I needed to talk to the Necrolord. Chasing her wasn't accomplishing anything, yet I had a feeling that diplomacy could somehow bring her out of hiding. And failing that, it could be used to at least trick her into weakening her grip on the city.

Looming over all my strategizing, however, was the fact that the Council couldn't be trusted. But I still needed to give them results.

I opened one of the videos Drake had sent me. Security camera footage from a week or two back. The wight, staring at the camera, as flesh puppets ravaged a grocery shop.

The wight, who called himself The Marshal, always stared at the camera. And as I stared right back at him, I could have sworn he was looking right at me. Not just any viewer, but at me. As if he was trying to tell me something. Or…was giving me an invitation.

"I know what she wants," I whispered.

"What?" Treth whispered back, even though he did not have to.

I stood up and began looking for a piece of paper and a marker.

"The wight said I'm allies with the Necrolord. And they have had plenty of chances to kill me. More than that, she helped me find Trudie. She wants…me."

"She could just kidnap you. Had the chance plenty of times."

"Not like that." I found paper and a black marker and began writing. "She wants me to come willingly. Of my own accord. She wants to strike a deal. She did it before. With the Cartel. It's her way of doing things."

"Her way of doing things is slaughter."

"But, even evil has its own code."

I ran to the window with the paper, stopping and holding it against the glass, facing outward.

"Message me." The sign said. I withdrew it after a minute. And sat down.

"Now, we wait."

"For what?"

"You'll see."

Treth didn't like that, and I couldn't blame him. We'd never tried to contact a necromancer before. Wasn't good business. And I really doubted that James and the police would like it if they found out. But I didn't feel like I had a choice. I needed to break this stalemate, and I needed to find out what was going on with Whiteshield, the Council, and C. Evergreen. If that meant talking to my enemy and risking the wrath of the people I'm sure killed Drake, then so be it.

But there was another problem. While I was pretty sure that the Necrolord was watching my apartment with her undead birds, there was no guarantee. My paranoia may be wrong, and the Necrolord may see no reason to keep a watch on me. But I doubted that. The Marshal had made it seem like I was the Necrolord's priority. She must be watching me. But would she contact me?

The waiting stretched, longer and longer, and I couldn't bring myself to read, to watch anything, or even chat to Duer, who shook his head pityingly at me as he flew to his birdhouse. How should I feel knowing a pixie refugee pitied me? I sat on my couch, in silence, watching the black screen of my cell phone.

Finally, it came. An unknown number. I hesitated, but then opened my phone to read the message.

"It is about time, Kitty Kat. I've been waiting."

Even though it was just text, I couldn't help but feel sick to my stomach. A monster had typed this. The person who I'd been hunting. Who had killed so many people. And I needed to reply.

"What should I say?" I whispered to Treth.

"Don't ask me. This wasn't my idea." He sounded like he shared my sentiments. We seldom spoke to the enemy. And only ever did so mockingly.

"I would like to make a deal," I wrote, and then paused. What was I doing? This was way too risky.

But was there any other way?

I thought about the Council's threats, Drake's body, and all my friends. It wasn't only the Necrolord I had to fear now. I had to do this.

"I would like to make a deal. I challenge your champion, The Marshal, in single combat in an open area.

If I win, you will reveal yourself to me in person. If I lose, I will be dead, and you can…"

"Kat!" Treth cried, as he read over what I was typing.

"It's the only way!" I whispered at him. The desperation in my voice must've been obvious, as Duer poked his head out.

"What's wrong, Kat?"

I looked at him and tried to smile. "Nothing, Duer. Good night."

He shook his head, pitying me again, and then disappeared inside his little home. I sometimes wondered what kept Duer here. What did he think of me?

"You can't do this, Kat," Treth tried to argue with me.

"I can." I finished the message and pressed send. "And I will."

I felt abject horror resonate from Treth, as we waited for a reply. The reply finally came.

"Sounds delightful. Time and place?"

"The abandoned stadium in Athlone. Saturday. 4pm."

"That's tomorrow," Treth said.

"No point delaying it."

Another message. "Accepted, Kitty Kat. Best of luck. And may this duel be honourable and enlightening."

I didn't respond after that. Enlightening? Odd.

"You could die," Treth whispered.

"I could. But I won't."

"How can you be so sure?"

"She doesn't want me dead. And her servant will fulfil her wishes with all his undying unbreath. He will let me kill him rather than remove his master's prize. She only allows this because she enjoys the theatrics."

"Or, because she does want you dead. But dead in such a way that she can use your body for her experiments."

"If that was her goal, she could have done it already. She wants me to trust her. She accepted this because she feels it will make me trust her."

"And? Will you?"

I looked out the window while stroking Alex, who had just jumped onto my lap. The darkness hid undead eyes. I just knew it.

"I will never trust a necromancer, Treth. But I will trust my manipulations of them."

"They're evil, not stupid."

"Never said they're stupid. But, I can try to understand them. And if I can do that, I can kill them."

"Or become them."

"Never…" I started, loudly and with venom in my voice. I shook my head. It wasn't worth it. "Please. Don't say something like that."

"I'm sorry, Kat. I know. You know I do. I'm just…I'm scared for you. For us. Let's say I've grown accustomed to my abode by now."

"Hah! Don't get too comfortable. After things calm down, we're gonna start looking for a way for you to get your own body."

"Wanting more privacy?"

I laughed, feeling a bit of levity. Alex purred, and I scratched him more behind the ears.

"That. But also, I feel you need some too. It's getting a bit crowded in here. For both of us. And you must be missing your old body, right?"

I felt Treth shrug. "It is what it is."

"Fatalist."

He laughed, and I joined in.

"Look at us," I finally said. "Possibly the hardest battle of our life tomorrow, and we're giddy."

"Hardest? Don't tell me you've forgotten the archdemon."

"Okay, one of the hardest. Or maybe not even that. We've killed plenty of wights before. The Marshal won't be any different."

I said that, but I didn't really believe it.

Cryomancy. Necromancy. Swordplay, if the rapier by his side was not just for show. Would I be good enough?

I'd have to be.

Chapter 20.   Duel

The hardest thing I had to do next was convince James that my plan was for the best. If he was in on the conspiracy or not, he still held the keys to my participation in the case. He accused me of treason when he heard that I'd negotiated with the Necrolord. I told him I'd do what it takes to finish the case. He called me an idiot who was throwing her life away. I told him to trust me.

Finally, he conceded and let me go, barring guards from helping me, as was my agreement with the Necrolord. I didn't doubt he'd have snipers in reserve, however. That's how cops functioned. Question was if they'd have their sights on the wight...or me.

I didn't tell my friends, even Brett and Guy, where I was going. I only left a note with Duer, for Colin. He was to give it to him if I died. Duer couldn't read (that well, at least), so I didn't fear him reading it himself.

I checked over my kit for the final time. My salamander coat, enchanted plate-mask, seax, dusack, wakizashi, Voidshot, six packs of Demanzite, combat padded-chest plate, and a stick of mint gum. It would be enough. It had to be.

James met me outside the abandoned stadium, surrounded by armed policemen.

"Are you sure about this?" he asked.

I ignored the question. "Is he here?"

James grimaced. "He is. Standing in there like a fucking grey mannequin from a renaissance fair."

I nodded and walked past him. He grabbed my shoulder.

"Don't do this if you think you can't win," he said, and I saw real concern in his eyes.

James was an asshole, but right then I didn't think he was involved in Drake's murder. He was an honest cop in a dishonest city. If I didn't do this, he may be next.

I nodded, and continued into the dark tunnel, leading into the stadium. My footsteps echoed in the dark, stenching tunnel, punctuating my heartbeats. I heard the clink of my gun on my belt and the rattle of its silver chain. I smelled the oil on my swords, the urine in the ditches, and the faint burning of my coat, smelling like a woodfire.

And then I smelled wet grass and felt sunlight on my skin.

The Marshal stood in the centre of what was once a soccer field. Deathly still. Waiting. The grass was overgrown in some places, dead in others. The goals had since rusted away, leaving brown metal husks protruding from the ground. Some of the plastic seats in the stadium had survived. I doubted there'd be any spectators using them for this show.

I took a deep breath.

"Are you sure about this?"

I was about to reply, but realised Treth hadn't asked that. I had. I nodded and went forward.

The Marshal was wearing his usual get-up. Rapier. Platemail cuirass. Feathered hat. His eyes were closed. Well, not exactly closed. They were eyeless holes, but there were no blue flames of undead sentience in them.

I stopped, ten metres from him, and the blue flames sparked. He cocked his head.

"You came," it, he, whatever, croaked, lipless and scratchy. Like evil sandpaper.

"I said I would."

The Marshal inclined his head.

"There's snipers somewhere here," I said, even though I felt Treth's displeasure. "I could not stop them, but I have a feeling they won't bother us."

A flicker of the flame suggested that he was glancing around.

"Thank you…Drummond. For your honesty. It is…rare. Unexpected."

We stood, facing off. Neither of us drew our weapons.

"Do you wish to fight now?" he asked, but he made no move towards his weapon, and did not raise his hand to use his magic.

I didn't reply or make a move to my weapons.

"If we are not to fight immediately, Drummond, I would like to talk."

My silence must have been good enough an affirmation for him.

"You remind me, Drummond, of a warrior I met in life. A long time ago. Far from here. He was a foreign man, to me, but I was a foreigner in his land. Before I met him, I did not truly understand honour, nor the true intensity and importance of battle. I was just a merchant's son, with an expensive sword and the mandate of the crown. I travelled across the world. Not for my country, as was the official reasoning, but...for myself. A... *desejo de viajar*. I learnt very little in my travels. We found lands. We explored them. We put up crosses to mark the land for the Lord, and then we continued our voyage. It didn't strike me as anything important...until I met this man. He called himself a *bushi*. A swordsman. I thought he was a barbarian, with strange hair, strange eyes, and strange ways. I thought him like the nobles of my home. All talk. No fight. But then...I saw this man fight... and kill. And I finally learnt something. I learnt that battle wasn't just a story. It was an art. A way of life. As the French would say: a *raison d'être*. I studied under him, for a while, and he taught me many things. Not so much about swordplay, but about why one fights. And what one loses."

The Marshal cocked his head at me, studying me like a predator would prey.

"Why do you fight, Drummond? Is it because you have nothing to truly lose?"

"If I don't fight, I lose everything," I said, without hesitation.

"A warrior's spirit," he replied, and his eyes glowed more intensely. "You would have liked my mentor. He could have taught you *bushido* better than I."

I drew my blades, both of them. Voidshot wouldn't help me much against a wight. Undead tended to shrug off bullets. Even void-touched, silver rounds.

The Marshal nodded, understandingly.

"It was…pleasant to talk to you, Drummond, even if you did not respond. I still find you disrespectful, but my mistress has never been wrong. You will do great things."

"Let's start on those great things," I said, tensing my grip and slowly moving into a fighting stance. "Beheading you will be a fine start."

Before he could respond, I charged him, holding my wakizashi ahead like a shield, and my dusack pulled back for a thrust. He didn't move his feet, but brought his hand down, chopping the air. My wakizashi, protected by its enchantments, took the brunt of a blast of frost, but I still dove to the side. I felt the chill through the metal and hand-wrap, as it shocked through my arm. Who would think ice could feel like electricity? I almost dropped the blade instinctively, but I held on. Even at the risk of frost-bite. Those wounds could be fixed. But only if I won.

I brought my wakizashi up again, managing to bat away a shard of ice the size of a dagger.

"You sure he doesn't mean to kill you?" Treth asked, his worry barely hidden beneath his sarcasm.

I wasn't so sure anymore.

I ducked low, making myself a smaller target, while darting towards him. He still hadn't drawn his blade, and the tips of his fingers were an icy blue. He pointed at me and I slid across the grass, the patch I'd previously been standing on turned into an ice patch.

I needed to disable his cryomancy. I reached for a pouch of demanzite in my breast-pocket, holding it in the same hand as my dusack. I shook it, feeling the crystalline dust inside heat up. The Marshal may be undead, but demanzite targeted spark. It didn't care about organic faculties. If the wight was casting, he'd be stunned.

The problem was: how would I get close enough to toss the stuff on him?

"No point dodging all day, Drummond," the Marshal shouted, over the icy-crack of another volley of shards, one that nicked my coat, releasing a hiss of steam as my coat responded with fiery rage. It didn't like ice. "I can do this for years. I have been doing this for years. You cannot outlast the dead."

I gritted my teeth and rolled to the side. The thud of shards into the grass sounded like bullets.

Couldn't outlast the dead?

I'd been outlasting the dead all my life.

I anticipated his next volley, charged to the right and, when he shot in that direction, I swerved to the left, missing his projectiles by a large margin.

He moved his feet. It was subtle, but he moved. That meant I'd done something right.

The Marshal pushed against the air, releasing a contained blizzard towards me, strafing across the ground. I couldn't duck below it, so I jumped right over. While I was in mid-air, he released a veritable machine-gun spray of tiny shards of ice, like a hundred needles. I ducked my head low and pirouetted in mid-air, taking the brunt of the force on my coat. The flames engulfed the needles, but I still felt many pin-pricks on my back. Phantoms of the actual projectiles.

Thank Conrad I had this jacket!

I landed on the grass with an oomph, expecting another volley to come my way while I lay prone. None came.

"I won't attack while you're down, Drummond, but others will not be so courteous."

I glanced towards him and caught a view of his feet. They were spread apart. Around five metres away. He wasn't standing impassively anymore. He was ready to fight properly.

The demanzite was still in my hand. It felt like I was holding a hot-water bottle. I needed to release it.

I hit the ground with the pommel of my wakizashi, lifting myself up. I looked towards the Marshal. He nodded, with respect. As if recognising me as a warrior. I could have laughed. I hadn't even cut him yet, and I was already panting and covered with bruises. Some warrior.

I charged, letting out a deep war cry, attempting to invigorate myself more than scare him.

He raised his hands to release more ice magic, and I twisted, putting my back towards him so the fire cloak would take the brunt of the force. I felt the projectiles hit, and without breaking stride, completed my rotation and continued the charge, only wobbling on my feet just a bit.

I needed to get the demanzite on him. I could feel it burning through my gloves. I'd never realised it was this volatile.

He was within striking distance, and I shot out with a thrust from my wakizashi, which he dodged. I felt the temperature drop around his hand. Now was my chance.

I slashed with my wakizashi as a feint, while bringing the bag of demanzite to my teeth, ripping its paper sachet open. My wakizashi didn't make contact as he seamlessly moved to the side. He was nimbler than any wight I'd fought before. But the bag was open. His hand glowed blue. I could practically feel his spark filling the air. It was now or never. I dove forward towards him, wakizashi thrusting and dusack slicing, my demanzite sachet hidden in my hand.

I felt my wakizashi bite into dry, ancient flesh, felt the resistance of bone and the satisfactory squelching emanate up my blade arm. The demanzite left its sachet, but the dusack hit something solid, glancing off, sending a shock up to my shoulder. Ice and water hit my jacket, creating a fog of steam around us. I could only see the twin blue-fiery eyes of the wight before me. A hand-span away.

I held my stance, panting. My dusack arm was recovering from its blow, and I continued to twist my wakizashi in its wound. The fog cleared, and I couldn't help but swear.

The demanzite crystals were frozen in a sheet of ice, floating between the wight's face and where my dusack had been. And the point of his rapier was facing my mask. I ducked but was too late. The sheet of ice hit me squarely in my face-plate, knocking me to the ground. It was followed by a barrage of frost that caused the worst brain freeze I'd ever felt. Like I'd stuck my head in a blizzard after a cold shower.

I rolled over, allowing the flames from my coat to absorb some of the impact and nullify it. I hoped the onslaught would stop now that I was lying down. The Marshal had said he wouldn't attack me while I was grounded, but I didn't really trust something that should've been dead. I heard the hiss of ice melting on my fire, while I crawled, giving myself some room to rise.

I tried to stand up but saw, just in front of me, a pair of black boots. In a flash, he'd appeared before me. I looked up at him and he looked down on me, his rapier held with one hand, levelled against my face-plate. With a sharp flick of his sword, I felt my face-plate crack. It had been frozen too much, and with a final blow, shattered.

I closed my eyes, avoiding icy metal shards falling into my eyes, while I lashed out towards his ankles. My blades didn't make contact as he backed away.

"Even on the ground, you are still in the fight, Drummond."

He flicked his rapier towards me and caught my cheek, opening it. I didn't cry out but wanted to. At least the blood was warm on my freezing skin.

"I...thought you said you wouldn't attack me on the ground," I said, trying to distract him as I attempted to find better footing.

"Never trust an enemy, Drummond. You know that."

In a blur, he was right before me. I lifted my arm in time to block a slash of his rapier. The cut didn't penetrate my padded arm-guard, but I still felt the blow. That wasn't the worst of it, though, as he blasted my foot with ice, pinning me to the ground.

I tried to pull my foot out of the block of ice, but it had firmly rooted me to the ground.

Well, now I was fucked.

"Right side," Treth called.

I lashed out to the right with my wakizashi, while ducking down. My blade parried away his, he backed away and stared me up and down.

"Impressive reflexes, Drummond. Very impressive for someone of your age. It is as if you had another pair of eyes."

I ignored him and whispered to Treth. "Any ideas?"

"I thought you said he wasn't going to kill us."

"I'd ask if you were praying," the Marshal said, walking carefully and calculatedly towards us. "But I know your lack of faith. But...who am I to judge? When I lived faithfully in life, I lost that faith in death. For you, it may be the reverse."

I ignored him. "There has to be a way, Treth."

I felt Treth shake his head. "I don't know, Kat. This isn't my type of fight. You know that. I was trusting you to get us out of here."

"Some help you are," I hissed, but he felt that I didn't mean it that way.

I tried to pull my foot from the ice block and felt no give. It was like solid rock. I ducked just in time as the

Marshal's sword slashed where my head had just been. He backed off and just looked at me from afar. Sizing me up. He paced up and down, considering me like a wolf would a wounded deer that was still bucking.

I had come into this fight prepared for a fight to the death, even though I believed that the Marshal would spare me for his mistress. There was always a chance I was wrong, and there was always a chance that the Necrolord would change her mind. Perhaps, all she wanted was this confrontation?

My eyes widened. Was this what the Necrolord wanted? She could have killed me before. Could have left me for dead before. But that was too simple. For all her tricks, perhaps she wanted to end me on the field of battle. Her champion versus me. This wasn't a charade. It was a real fight to the death. And I'd let my hubris allow me to think that I understood the Necrolord.

The Marshal feinted forward, and I brought up my defence. He laughed and continued his pacing, extending it into a circle around me.

"Treth," I whispered, anxious. "What do I do?"

Before he could answer, the Marshal spoke.

"Do you know the primary teaching of *bushido*?"

"Striking fast, and all that," I guessed, attempting to keep him talking so I could figure a way out of this. I thought the ice would melt, but it was still rock solid. Like a glacier around my foot and ankle.

He shook his head. "The core principle of *bushido*, the lesson that drives its entire teaching is an acceptance of death. For that is the warrior's path."

He stopped and looked me in the eyes from across the tract of grass.

"You are a warrior, Drummond. And your time will come, one day. And you will need to accept it when it does."

Accept death?

My own. Perhaps. But others? My parents? My friends? All the innocents? Death was a fact of life. But didn't mean I had to like it. Not for me, and not for anyone else.

I felt anger rise. Why should I accept death? Why accept the end when I had so much to live for? And why make sacrifices so I could keep living?

"Bullshit," I whispered, through gritted teeth. No. I couldn't accept death.

The Marshal whipped his rapier to the side with a flourish, audibly cutting the air.

"Curse all you wish, but ponder it, Drummond. You have come far down the warrior's path. Yet, there is so much more for you to learn."

"It's rich coming from an undead that one should accept death," I spat.

His blue-flame eye flickered. "Yet, the dead can die again. And I accept this...It is time for you to do the same."

He waited. And I faced him. I like to think that I did so defiantly. Eyes unwavering. But it didn't do me any good. I felt tears. And the coldness of rain on my unmasked face and head. I smelled and tasted iron, and the now wet dirt. The Marshal's eyes wavered, blue flames in the wind. The feather in his hat was sodden, drooping downward. Every drop that hit my coat hissed and went up into steam.

I felt Treth's resignation. He had faced death before. He knew how it felt. He felt it coming.

But I had looked death in the eyes before. And it had not taken me yet.

"Come kill me, wight."

The Marshal shook his head, disappointed. "If only we had more time, Drummond. Then perhaps you would have been a better warrior. But this world doesn't give us enough time…only wasted opportunities."

The Marshal broke his circling of me and charged me dead-on. His footfalls squelched on the soil and grass. I didn't raise my swords in defence. I held them limp by my sides, and I collapsed to my knees.

"Kat!" Treth yelled.

The Marshal closed the gap in a grey blur with blue eyes, his sword raised above his head, ready to slash my throat. I wouldn't give him the chance.

Pulling my foot from the ice was the most painful thing I've ever done. More painful even than the brutalising I'd received from the archdemon. I felt every bit of skin rip, ever nerve scream and my bones consider breaking. Still, I pushed off, pulling my foot from its enclosure. And with both my feet free, I ducked my head under the wight's slash, and tackled his midriff, using my blades to spit his legs. I grunted as he slashed at the backs of my legs, but before he could do anything worse, I lifted him over my shoulders and, with his weight, fell backwards so that my coat was covering his vital areas.

I whispered, "Burn."

And my coat engulfed him. Wights could feel pain, and the Marshal screamed. I did not stop. I pushed every ounce of will into the flames. It couldn't be merely a stinging heat. It needed to immolate the wight to cinders. To end him. I pushed the coat to its limit, until it sputtered and stopped. I felt the almost conscious presence in the coat die, extinguished as I pushed it too far.

The roar of flames stopped, and I no longer felt the wight squirming. I rolled until I was on my stomach and used my blades to lift myself to my knees. I buckled and cried out. My legs had been cut to ribbons, only adding to the pain in my frost-scorched foot.

The Marshal lay blackened and almost crushed by my side. His eyes still flickered faintly, and his sword hand twitched. I didn't hesitate to chop the arm off at the shoulder. It twitched no more.

I thrust my dusack into the wight's other hand, pinning it to the ground, and used it to bring myself to a knee, despite the pain. I winced, but the adrenaline still allowed me to persevere.

The wight's eyes were still a flaming blue.

"Drummond…" he rasped.

I considered beheading him now, but something stayed my hand.

"You accepted your death," he said. "At that final moment. You didn't raise your weapons."

"No. I feinted."

The wight nodded, and I caught a curl of his lipless mouth. It looked almost like a grin.

"I did not understand why the mistress respected you so, Drummond. But I know, now. You will be the one to defeat her enemies."

"I will defeat HER."

The wight's eyes flickered. "You are being used, Kat Drummond."

"So is any tool, and I am a willing sword to strike down monsters."

"Yet, you serve them."

That stopped me.

The glow of his eyes began to fade. "I am honoured that you bested me, Monster Hunter. Continue to be just that. Slay monsters. The dead and the living."

"I will."

"Then, I have left my mistress in good hands."

Before I could press him further, the flames in his eyes disappeared, and what was left of his body slumped. There was no more sense of agency in the lump of dried flesh.

It began raining in earnest and I didn't hear the hiss of the droplets hitting my enflamed coat.

"Thank you," I said, and I meant it. I would be dead without this coat. And it had died for me.

I didn't behead the Marshal in the end. I let him lie there, on the field, with full knowledge he did not intend to return.

With both my swords, I began the slow crawl home, unable to rise to my feet, as the rain pelted down on me, and the sky darkened despite my victory.

Chapter 21.   Politics

My challenging the Marshal was never intended to draw out the Necrolord, but it was always a planned bonus. My entire goal was to eliminate the Necrolord's key lieutenant, slowing down her slaughter. If she decided to honour the deal, then that would be great, but it wasn't my primary goal. I needed to slow down her campaign, and I needed to save innocent lives. I was hoping that would have convinced the Council that we were making progress.

James did not find this argument compelling, as he shouted at me from across his office, while I stood using crutches, my legs still recovering from their injuries. The Necrolord had not revealed herself, as was the agreement, and the Council found the consolation prize not worth the trouble.

"You told us that the Necrolord would reveal herself if you won the duel!" James shouted.

"I cannot be held responsible for her actions. What matters is that her lieutenant has been eliminated. The vast majority of her operations were led by the wight. Without him, she is severely hamstrung."

"That wasn't the deal, Drummond," he hissed through gritted teeth. "The Council wants the Necrolord. The death of one monster isn't worth the bureaucratic mess your stunt caused."

I shrugged. "I made the deal with the Necrolord to flush out her lieutenant. If she honoured the deal, then great. She did not, but we still got a prize."

"So, you were bait?"

"Bait seldom fights back," I said, but I still felt like bait.

James sighed. "Why didn't you tell us? We would have provided fire support if the goal was to just kill the wight."

"Would the Council have allowed that?" I retorted.

That stung him. He knew what his bosses were like. They wouldn't have permitted a police operation against what they believed was a non-threat.

"Even if you fired, it wouldn't have helped," I added. "He could shrug off most rounds, and even the best sniper may have hit me."

James rubbed his head and considered his empty coffee mug. I could go for some coffee. It had been a long day. My stint at the hospital had been short, at least. My legs needed to recover, but I didn't need to be bedridden for them to do so. I was also trying to save on medical bills. Healing magic was expensive. Better to recover naturally if I could.

"James," I said, trying to use my most diplomatic tone. "The wight killed countless people. Drake's intelligence suggests that he was crucial to the Necrolord's campaign. Without him, a lot of innocent people have been avenged and many more can sleep more soundly at night."

I waited for his response, as he looked longingly into his empty mug.

"That's got to count for something!"

James looked up and I could see sadness in his eyes. Sadness. Fatigue. And faintly, guilt.

"I'm sorry, Drummond. The Council is clear on this. They want the Necrolord. They don't care about her projects. They want HER."

"So, it's not about saving people?"

His hand tensed on the desk. I advanced, bringing myself closer. Despite my crutches, I still summoned my usual air of menace.

"What about every other monster in this city, Montague? What about the other necromancers? The gangsters? The demons? The vampires? Do none of them matter?"

"Our orders are clear," James said, through gritted teeth. His words sounded rehearsed. As if he had been repeating them to himself. "The Necrolord is the priority. No distractions. No other operations."

A heavy silence fell on the office. I was about to respond but shook my head.

"I will contact you with data if more becomes available," James said, in a dismissive tone. He looked down at his computer. I turned and left.

"How can these men pretend that they serve the people?" Treth asked, out of earshot of anyone as I exited into an empty, dimly lit hallway with grey linoleum flooring. Government buildings were just as drab on the inside as they were on the outside.

"It seems they aren't even pretending, anymore." I tried to sound heated but failed. All I felt was my exertions, planning, injuries and anxieties piling up. I was tired. Too tired to care about my victory or my defeat. I was even too tired to rage at the Council's injustice.

I needed a rest. A rest from this case, and from working with employers who didn't care about saving lives.

My phone rang, and I leant up against the wall, so I could answer it.

"Hey, Pranish," I said, trying to sound upbeat.

"Drained already? It's only Wednesday."

Oh yeah. He didn't know about my injuries. Only Colin did. I managed to convince him that it was actually much less serious than many of my other injuries. I must admit that I did almost cry when he asked why my coat wasn't igniting anything anymore. I'd only had it for a few months, but I had worn it more than anything else in that time. I knew it was just a coat, but I had a connection to it. And now it was dead. I couldn't help but wonder if I shouldn't have pushed it so hard.

"Work," I said, hoping he wouldn't press. I wasn't only tired of work. I was tired of talking about it.

"Anyway, Kat, two things. First, my little project is nearing completion."

"Great!" I said, managing to gather up some genuine enthusiasm. I knew this meant a lot to both Pranish and Colin.

"I knew you'd be excited. Means I won't keep hogging Colin."

"He has enjoyed working with you. I think he'll be sad that it's over. But excited that it's done."

"Heh. Admit it, Kat. You're gonna be glad that you get to spend more time with him."

I didn't deny it.

"Anyway, to celebrate the completion of the working model, I am having a bit of a get-together at my place this Friday. Snacks, drinks, etcetera. I want to demonstrate the project to you guys."

I was sensing a but...

"What's the second thing?" I asked.

"It's about Andy. Been thinking more about what you told me, and it's been making me angry."

"Good."

"Sure, sure. I know you thrive in your sea of rage..."

Damn straight, I did.

"But this isn't some monster you can slay. Trudie is our friend. A deluded friend, but our friend all the same. Has Andy called you after?"

"No, but…" my hands tensed when I remembered Oliver. "His crony, Oliver, threatened Colin."

"What?!"

"A week back. Told me that if I didn't date Andy, then something may happen to Colin."

"What fucking weirdos. What did you do?"

"I told him in polite, legally deniable ways, that I'd kill him if he came near to Colin."

"Classic Kat. How did Colin handle it?"

Not well. Well, he handled it well, but not my proposed solution. I didn't say this of course. Talking about illegal firearms in a police station was not the best idea, even if I had just been joking about murder.

"He took it in his stride. Much calmer than I am about these sorts of things."

"Believe me, he lets his anxieties flow readily when he can. He decides to act all manly only when he's around you."

"Hey! You're one to talk."

"Looking for a fight, bub?" Pranish's tone belied his amusement. I was glad he seemed to be back to his old self. "So, with this party on Friday, I really want Trudie to be there, but she'll insist on bringing Andy."

"Easy. We ignore him like we always do. Even he can't be stupid enough to misbehave in your home surrounded by people."

"It's more than that, Kat." Pranish sounded serious now, and hesitant. As if he was making up his mind here and now. "I think we should tell Trudie what's up, and…"

"Confess your undying love for her?" I chided.

He didn't get the joke. "Yes."

"Oh, gods, Pranish. You like to live dangerously, don't you?"

"Now look who's talking."

He paused, and I heard Colin on the other side calling Pranish to look at some sort of gibberish.

"Send Colin my greetings," I said.

"I'm gonna tell him you miss his scent," Pranish chuckled, mischievously. I laughed. It was good to have my friend back.

He hung up.

"A party?" Treth asked. "Would be a nice change of pace."

"I remember when you wanted me to hunt zombies every waking hour."

"Let's say that I've matured. Even I'm getting tired, and I don't even have a body to get tired."

"We do deserve a rest."

I glanced at James' office door.

"Even if they don't seem to think so."

"You did good, Kat. Really good. I really thought you'd have to sacrifice your foot there."

"I get the feeling that my fighting style is a lot more agile than yours was, my knightly friend."

"Definitely. I could never pull that off in my plate mail. I would have fallen to the earth, and then waited for him to finish me off."

"Tell me…how did you guys last so long in such heavy armour?"

"It had its uses. Enchanted with purification magic, it could also resist necromantic attacks. We used different strategies. Strategies that wouldn't work with you or here. You don't have much in the way of a phalanx, and your compatriots seem keener on using guns than maces, axes and blades."

"Alas, but I'll show them the way."

"You seem to be in higher spirits."

"Do I?"

"A touch more energetic."

"Really? Well, maybe I'm looking forward to the party."

"Not just that," Treth said, and I felt his invisible examining gaze. "It feels like a weight has been lifted. At least a small one. Perhaps, because of the slaying of the Marshal."

"You mean the wight?"

"Yeah."

"Didn't think you'd call him by his title. He's an undead."

"I know, I know. And we both have reason to despise them…but he was different."

"He killed hundreds of people."

"Yet, we despise zombies that kill none. There was something peculiar about that wight. I don't think he was lying to us."

"So, we should trust his mistress? We should serve the Necrolord?"

"Don't speak so loudly! You're still in the belly of the beast."

I looked around. The halls were empty, but walls could be thin. I knew that these cops were meant to be my allies, but I couldn't help but agree with Treth here. I did feel like I was in the belly of the beast. Perhaps, the enemy of my enemy wasn't always my friend. Especially if they had, as I suspected, killed Drake.

"Discussing this now serves little purpose. Let's go home, Treth."

I felt him nod, and I proceeded to the elevator. It was shaky, and I almost regretted not taking the stairs, despite my leg. Finally, I reached the ground floor and exited the station, just to run into Brett.

"Hey, Kats!" he grinned ear to ear. He was in civvies. I seldom saw him without his tactical vest and strapped up with all manner of firearms. He was wearing a Metallica t-shirt, dark jeans and his usual combat boots. I saw a slight indentation in his pants where I suspected he was carrying a concealed pistol.

"Brett!" I said, with some genuine pleasure. I did like Brett, despite my misgivings about him earlier in the year. "What are you doing so close to the ticks?"

263

I winced at my own casual insult of the cops – especially as two walked past me. Bad, Kat. Bad! Have some self-control.

"Drakenbane needed me to deliver some dossiers."

"Errand boy now? Finally got that promotion!"

"Hur hur," he feigned amusement, while being amused. "What are you doing here?"

"Getting my ear blasted off for eliminating a threat to Hope City."

"So, typical politics?"

"Pretty much."

"Anyway," Brett said. "Need a lift home? Can't have you riding your bike with those legs. What happened to them? Becoming a mummy?"

"Made a sacrifice."

"Fine. Don't tell me." He grinned.

I followed him to his car and got in, with his aid. He could be the gentleman when he wanted to be, it seemed. I could readily admit that without blushing. I had my heart set on Colin. It was kinda nice committing myself. Meant I didn't need to make hard decisions anymore.

"So…" he started, as he pulled out of his parking space and got onto the street. "Guy, Cindy and I are going shooting with some full-autos this Friday. Some CDF issue stuff. Should be fun. You're welcome to come."

"Friday? What time?"

I didn't want to snub him again, but I'd committed to Pranish's party.

"Evening."

"Shit. Got Pranish's party. He's celebrating the first working model of his thingamajig."

"Congrats to him! Even though I still don't know what it's for."

"Contracts and stuff."

We stopped talking and I felt a melancholic silence descend on the vehicle. I really hoped Brett didn't feel snubbed. He was my friend, after all. And he'd stood up for me quite a lot over the last month.

"You able to shoot on Saturday?" I asked. "Even if the full-autos aren't available, should still be fun."

"Well, yeah…I can shift some stuff around…but might be difficult…"

I felt a bit of anxiety arise from his stalling, but then he grinned at me.

"Of course. We'll get the machine-pistols out. Guy won't mind."

"Great!" I felt a sense of joy at ensuring I didn't let my friend down, and firing someone else's ammunition was always fun. Despite James' earful, things seemed to be looking up. It was about damn time.

Chapter 22.   Love

I awoke on Thursday morning to no alarm, no frantic phone-calls, no gunshots and no screaming. Just the sun peeking through the curtains and the aroma of bacon and eggs. I knew I had class today, but I'd missed so much already, one day wasn't going to hurt me any more. It also seemed that Colin didn't need to go in to court today and that he used the opportunity to cook breakfast. There were benefits to dating. Definitely.

I got up and exited my bedroom. Colin had already made up his blankets and pillows from where he'd been sleeping on the couch. Yeah, we were dating, but we were also both a little bit shy. More from nerves than anything else. He'd been residing on my (he insists) more than comfortable enough couch, for the last while. Even after the debacle where I gave him the gun, he'd still stuck with me. Even though I didn't know why. Treth told me that he wanted to protect me. That confused me. It was me who always did the protecting. And while Colin had helped me in the past, would he truly be able to protect me? And could my voracious independence allow him to do that?

Well, I let him move in. I let him invade my sanctified personal space. If an introvert lets you into their home, then you are immensely privileged.

I yawned in greeting to Colin, who was wearing a "Kiss the Cook" apron over a t-shirt and jeans, despite just cooking breakfast. I obliged and planted a kiss on his cheek. Usually, such displays would leave me blushing, but I'd gotten used to that, if not more.

"No class today?"

I shrugged. He got the message.

He deposited some bacon, toast and egg onto a plate, which I considered, and then bit into. I wasn't used to breakfast, even though Colin had cooked for me for quite a few of the days while he had been living here. I hadn't eaten so well since I'd lived with Trudie's family. Even so, I still snuck in a cup of instant noodles every so often. While we were kinda living together, we both had our own lives and spent more time out of the house. Me on my hunts, him on his lawyering and working with Pranish.

"So...your thing with Pranish is complete?" I asked, my way of making small talk inbetween bites.

"Not really complete, but it's ready. Like, an alpha test version. We can start rolling it out to testers in lawmantic circles and see what they think of it."

"Think they'll like it?"

"I hope so. Pranish has put a lot into this. He deserves the recognition."

"And you."

He shrugged. "I just helped with this and that. You don't celebrate the translator. You celebrate the author. Pranish is the author."

"But he couldn't have done this without you."

We stood up, me chewing on some bacon and Colin considering me. Finally, he laughed.

"Okay. You win. I'll acknowledge that I may have helped. At least a little."

He joined me with his own meal and we ate, discussing this and that. It was pleasant, but I felt an uncomfortable topic looming that needed to be discussed, even though I did not want to. I didn't really discuss things that troubled me. When I did, I discussed them with Treth, who was basically me anyway. But I was troubled now, and I needed to discuss at least some of these topics with Colin.

He noticed that something was on my mind and placed his hand on mine.

"What's up?" he said, simply.

Well, where to start? Drake was dead. I think the government killed him. My nemesis thought me her greatest ally. I kinda regretted killing a wight. I didn't know if I was doing the right thing. I was going to fail second year and didn't care. I was sick of Whiteshield guarding my place but knew that a vampire bitch was hunting me because I murdered her boyfriend. My legs were still injured, and I needed a crutch to hobble along. Andy was being a creepy bastard. And Oliver was threatening to do something to Colin. And I had to see them this Friday, while celebrating my friend's and boyfriend's achievement – even if I still didn't really understand what it was. That my flaming coat was dead. And more than all of this, I didn't know how to proceed. I didn't know what to do, or how to feel about it. I was lost and in pain.

My lip quivered, and he reached over to me without hesitation, engulfing me in a hug.

"Where do I begin?" I asked, unable to stop a sob from coming out.

What was happening? I didn't do stuff like this? I didn't cry. Stoical to the end. Other people's protector. Never protected. I instinctively tried to pull away, but Treth stopped me.

"Let him protect you. In his own way."

I considered ignoring him and pulling away. To skulk into my own corner and cry by myself. To be unflappable in front of others, and to let these phases of weakness be only witnessed by Treth, Duer and my cat.

But Treth was right. Colin deserved this. And if I really felt the way I thought I did about him, then I needed to let him see this. To let him see the good, the bad, the sad and the unassailable dread that permeated my life.

I didn't hug back. It wasn't that type of hug. I collapsed, further and further into his arms, letting them envelop me. I let myself smell his cologne, while I wept into his shoulder. Pranish didn't realise how close to the truth his joke was. I did miss Colin's scent when he wasn't around.

Who could think this could happen to me? That I could find love among the monsters.

"You can talk to me if you'd like, Kat," Colin said. "Or not. You don't have to. But I can be here for you if you need me. I know your life is full of danger, and I worry for you. But I'm not going anywhere. Even if it means I have to bandage you up or hear about the monster that almost just…killed you…then I'm here."

"Aren't…" I sniffed through the tears. "Aren't you afraid we're taking things too fast? I don't…know if you understand what it means to be around me."

"I know enough." And I heard the certainty in his voice. "And while many things are uncertain, I am pretty sure that I love you, or will."

"Will?"

He laughed, quietly, and not so harshly, as I was still nestled into his shoulder.

"Don't want to risk taking things too fast, do we?"

I laughed too, and finally pulled myself from his shoulder.

"I got stuff on your shoulder," I said, embarrassed.

"It's fine." He offered me a hand and I accepted. I didn't need the crutches, as he let me put all my weight on him.

Could I really do this? Could I rely on someone else? Not just for a mission. Not like how I'd rely on Brett to hunt vampires, or Cindy to heal me up. Could I let Colin in? To help me in a way no one else except maybe Treth has before.

Colin helped me down onto the couch. I winced a bit as my mending wounds stung and felt his hesitation, but I indicated that I was okay. The bit of healing magic I received was marvellous, but not godly. I needed some time to recover. I wasn't looking forward to the scars when I was unbandaged.

"So, what's the plan for today?" Colin asked, taking a seat near me, but not so close as to risk nudging my injured legs.

"Not going into class. And the cops are angry with me, so no missions. You?"

"I left today open to work with Pranish on the thing, but it seems he doesn't need me today."

"So…"

We were alone. For the day. Alone, except for the Whiteshield guards outside. Well, the way they acted, they may as well be statues. We hadn't had a day alone since…ever. Always just stolen moments between work.

I felt nerves rise up simultaneously with another, less prudish sentiment. But what did I have to be nervous about it?

I looked at Colin, into his eyes, and I saw adoration. I didn't need to be nervous. I didn't need to doubt what he felt about me. And I didn't need to worry about anything else – if only for a little while.

A naughty grin crossed my face. Colin looked at it, confused, but then he smiled.

I leaned in, and then swore loudly.

"Legs?" he whispered.

"Yeah, sorry."

"Nah, I'll be more careful."

He tried to lean closer, avoiding my legs, but it was awkward. He could reach my lips, but it was not close enough for my liking.

"Fuck it," I said, and pulled him closer. I felt the pain in my legs as he brushed up against them by mistake, but I could deal with it. I'd felt much worse before.

We kissed for a while, and I felt Treth leave to his personal chamber. That only enticed me further.

"I want…" I began.

"Hmmm?"

"I…carry me…"

"Excuse me?"

"To the bedroom," I said, and even though I blushed, I looked him in the eyes. "Carry me to the bedroom."

He looked at me, discerning if I was being serious. Then he laughed. He stood up and I put my arms out, placing them around him as he lifted me up by my upper thighs, avoiding my injuries. He strained a bit, but then lifted me up. His face was one of extreme concentration. So, I ambushed him with a kiss. To his credit, he didn't drop me.

"Is her majesty pleased?" he said, in a mock haughty accent.

I laughed. "She is."

Colin closed the door behind us and, for at least a little while, I forgot all about the government, the monsters, and the pain.

Chapter 23.   The Party

I liked parties, even though I was undoubtably an introvert. There was just something about them that was appealing to even a cynical misanthrope like me. A sort of collective escapism and mutual joy. And while every party takes a different form, there was something special about them that allowed them to be more than just a gathering of people. A social construction that turned a group of people into something to remember.

"Are you sure you don't need any help?" Colin asked, concern crossing his brow. He was carrying a backpack with some last-minute stuff for Pranish, and a bottle of Saronsberg Shiraz.

I waved him off, while hobbling up the path to Pranish's apartment block. I only needed a single crutch now, to keep the pressure off my frost-scorched foot. The lacerations and other injuries had healed up nicely. Healing magic was a marvel! Kinda made it hard to care about the consequences of actions, though. At least, I still had my scars to remind me of every time I brushed up close to death. Scars and memories.

I accepted Colin's arm as he helped me up a step and we entered the elevator. I usually preferred the stairs, but I'm not so stubborn that I'd suffer the entire journey up to Pranish's floor just because I didn't trust a bit of pre-Cataclysm engineering.

"Pranish called ahead," Colin said. "Wants to go over some stuff before the party…"

I detected a hint of worry in his voice. I reached out and squeezed his hand.

"It'll be fine."

I smiled at him and he smiled back, squeezing my hand in response.

Would it be fine, though?

Andy was coming. And Trudie. I hadn't spoken to her since our fight.

"She's your best friend," Colin said, as if reading my mind. "I'm sure if you just talk to her, you'll sort everything out."

"I hope so." I frowned.

It wasn't just that, though. It was also Andy. I didn't like him and Colin being in the same room. Even if he didn't do anything really stupid, he was a bully. This was Colin and Pranish's night. I didn't want it ruined.

We arrived at Pranish's floor and got out. I was immediately relieved to be on a more solid, unmoving surface. Have I said how I don't like elevators?

Colin let go of my hand to knock on Pranish's door. I used the opportunity to straighten my dress. I decided it was time to wear a dress again. A black one that Trudie had picked out for me. Sure, it left my bandages uncovered, but everyone here knew my profession. The scars and all shouldn't come as a surprise.

"You're late." Pranish grinned. He was wearing a formal vest and tie over a white button-up shirt.

"We're twenty minutes early," I replied. "And this is Hope City. Two hours late is still early."

"Very true."

Pranish made some room for us to enter. His glass dining room table was covered with snacks and some drinks. Colin placed the wine on the table.

"I'm going to have to steal him away for just a bit," Pranish said.

"Sorry, Kat. We'll sort this out quick."

I nodded through a mouthful of cocktail sausage roll. But as Colin and Pranish disappeared around the corner, I felt renewed anxiety in my gut. I made my way to the bathroom and bent over the sink.

"Andy?" Treth asked.

I nodded.

"Don't stress, Kat. I'll be watching him. He won't be able to do anything without me noticing."

"Thanks, Treth…"

I felt him nod.

"Treth…" I whispered.

"Yes?"

"How…how are you doing?"

He laughed, shocking me, but then stopped. "Really?"

I nodded again. I was dead serious.

"I'm…fine, Kat. Fine as I can be. Fine as you are. Or maybe not as fine…"

"I mean…are you fine with what happened…last night…"

"Mercifully, I wasn't there. But…"

"But what?"

"I'm happy for you," he said, but I felt some hesitation.

Before I could ask anything further, I heard Pranish open the front door, and heard Trudie's voice. I gulped.

"She loves you, Kat. And you'll be friends again."

Treth paused.

"You better become friends, again, actually. Especially after what we went through to get her back."

I exited the bathroom, reluctantly. Trudie was alone by the snack table, considering the canapés. She was not as gothy as usual, rather opting for her semi-formal wear. More reasonable make up, with red lipstick and black mascara. She wore a red dress, longer than mine. But her boots were still her usual high-heeled combat boots. Typical Trudie. Even so, she looked more like a celebrity than a vampire. With my recent run-ins with vamps, I was glad about that.

Trudie didn't notice, or chose not to notice, me as I approached the table. I looked her up and down. She was impassive, but obviously ignoring me.

How long could this go on?

"Hey, Trudie…" I started. "How are…things?"

She looked at me and I saw a hint of irritation and anger. "We both hate small talk, Kats. Let's cut to the chase. I'm dating Andy. That's my choice. You had your shot. It's over. And this crap about him not saving me…he didn't have to save me and neither did you. That was your choice and it's unfair to beat him up about it. Not everyone can be as heroic as you. And not everyone needs to be as heroic as you. There's only one of you, Kat. And that's all I need."

She stopped for breath.

"Now. Can we be friends again?"

I paused, stunned, and then burst out laughing. I sensed shock from Treth, and Trudie's eyes widened. I hobbled towards her and dropped my crutch as I gave her a hug, that she resisted initially, but then returned.

"I missed you, Troodz."

"You haven't called me that in years."

"Like it?"

"I hate it."

"All the more reason to keep saying it."

We maintained the hug for a bit, until Trudie pulled back just a bit.

"You're using me as a crutch, aren't you?"

"That obvious?"

She laughed and picked up my crutch.

"Should I ask?" She indicated my injuries.

"You want the answer?"

"No."

I felt a weight lift as I patched things up with Trudie. We sat down on Pranish's couch and spoke about many things. None of them about Andy. But we did speak about Colin, and I told her everything. And I mean everything. She practically squealed with excitement. It was good to have my female friend back in my life. Don't get me wrong – the men are capable, but they lack a certain penchant for some topics.

Some party guests arrived and Trudie was assigned to let them in. Many of them were classmates of Trudie's and Pranish's. Some were actually Colin's friends. Eventually, the inevitable happened and Andy arrived, with Oliver in tow.

"What is he doing here?" I whispered to Treth.

"Makes no difference. I'll keep an eye on him as well," he responded.

What would I do without Treth? A thought crossed my mind. When would I tell Colin about Treth? How would he take it? I noted that I thought *when*, not *if*. Look at me. All love-struck. Already planning everything. Even something as intimate as telling my boyfriend that I have a knightly spirit from another world living in my head.

Still, as Andy glanced over Trudie's shoulder to look at me from across the room, I felt an acidity rise from my stomach. I had the urge to find Colin, wherever he was. To keep him safe. I didn't bring my swords, but my knife was still hidden inside my dress. And Voidshot was in my backpack, with Colin.

Along the way, I hobbled past motley groups of people. Some of whom I knew, and most others that I did not. Two I recognised from my own course in undead studies. Monster's rights advocates.

"Fae-catchers are dregs," the one, a girl nibbling on a vegetarian cocktail sandwich, said. I agreed with her 100%. Especially after befriending Duer, fae-catchers were one of the worst types of people for me.

"But you misunderstand the problem," her companion, a girl with a button on her lapel that looked like an X going through Drakenbanes' logo, replied. "Fae-catchers are just victims of a system that raises money above the lives of sentient beings. They are victims just as much as the faeries and pixies they kill. Money is the problem."

"Bullshit," I said, speaking before thinking. The two swivelled towards me. I felt embarrassed for a second, but then stood strong. "Plenty of people. Me, and you two I presume, don't go around killing fae for a quick buck. Fae-catching isn't the norm. It's the exception. Plenty of people make money without doing harm. It's not the system that's broken. It's some people that are just shit."

"But money creates a demand…"

"People create the demand. Money is a tool. Without it, some people would still kill fae and snort their flesh like cocaine. It isn't a desire for wealth that is evil, it is the willingness to hurt that is."

"Wait," one of them said, squinting at me. "Aren't you that part-time monster hunter?"

I saw Colin speaking to Pranish across the room, and immediately lost interest in the conversation. I heard the girl shout as I limped away.

"Your time will come, murderer. No life is worth a pay check."

Well, good thing I mostly killed dead things then.

"It will be fine," Colin said, the same way I said it to him.

"It's just...I need this to work," Pranish said, perspiration on his brow. No hint of his usual snark. Just worry that his work was going to fail.

"Worst case scenario – we fix the bug and continue," Colin smiled. I knew he was worried as well, but it wasn't time to show Pranish that anxiety. Colin knew the importance of putting on a confident facade. Lawyers might be stereotyped as dishonest, but sometimes that dishonesty had a time and place. I felt my affection for Colin grow three times as I saw him calming my friend.

"Worst case is that the entire thing is a bust."

"We tested it. It works."

"Yeah, Pranish," I said, butting in. "Get your game face on. We're right behind you."

"That'd be unfortunate," he said. "My back's gonna be up against the window. And it's a long drop."

"You know what I mean." I shoved him playfully, almost fell off my crutch, and was caught by Colin.

Pranish rolled his eyes.

"Not to separate you again, but can you set up the projector, Colin?"

"Sure, sure." He looked at me. "Save me a seat."

I gave him a light peck, and then turned to Pranish, who was back to his fretting.

"You gonna do it?" I asked.

"Do what?"

I inclined my head at Trudie, who was laughing with Andy near some people from their IT class.

"Ah…that. I…it depends."

"Depends on what?"

"If the presentation goes well."

"Why the fuck does that matter?"

I must've spoken loudly, as some nearby people looked my way.

Pranish moved closer and whispered.

"If this fails, I'm not going to be in the frame of mind to speak to her."

"That's just you being defeatist. If you succeed, you can use your high to muster the confidence to tell her. If you fail, then you can muster some sort of success from the evening. But I know it won't fail."

287

"How can you be so sure?"

"Because you're my friend, and he's my…because you two have worked too hard on this. And he said that you tested it. It won't fail. Not this far along."

Pranish looked about to argue, but smiled, and leant in for a friendly hug. I accepted.

"Thanks, Kat. And if the other thing, with Trudie, doesn't work out – promise me that things between us won't be weird."

"It's impossible for our lives to get any weirder."

"Pranish! It's ready," Colin called.

"Thanks!" Pranish said, releasing me. I hobbled behind him and found a place to sit. Most people were standing, but my injuries gave me a sort of privilege.

Once everyone was seated, Colin (who was sitting by the coffee table, which was shoved up below the window) pressed a switch, activating a hologram crystal that lit up with a PowerPoint display.

The title of the slide read: "Technologising Lawmancy."

It was finally time for me to figure out what this entire thing was about.

"We all know," Pranish began. "The limitations of the magical word and our technology. Since the Cataclysm, computers, cell phones and all off-shoots of those inventions have developed independently of the magical world. As if the Cataclysm never happened. When spells and computers have tried to merge, results have been less than stellar."

Pranish clicked the button on his remote, changing the slide to a picture of a burnt-out laptop.

"Only some gains have been made to merge the otherworldly with distinctly human technology. This display crystal being one of them. Otherwise, the industries of magic and technology have been distant. Not even rivals. One exists in a world where the Cataclysm never happened, and the other embraces only the Cataclysm. Until today."

Colin stood, handing Pranish two cell phones.

"We have been working on a way of digitising lawmantic contracts, so that court lawmancers, excessive legal fees, and maybe even judges and courts are no longer needed in the future. On these cell phones is an app we are currently calling *DigiLaw*. Through this app, willing parties can sign contracts without the need for a lawmancer, so to compel the consenting parties to undertake the agreed upon contract. Lawmancy has been a huge innovation in the enforcement of contracts, but the costs of a lawmancer have, in the past, been exorbitant. *DigiLaw* aims to change that."

He indicated at Trudie. "Will you help demonstrate the app, Trudie?"

A terrible thought crossed my mind. Was he going to use this app to confess to Trudie? In front of all these people?

Oh gods. What were you thinking, Pranish?

"Well, using it hands-on might help me understand it," Trudie grinned, and stood up. Pranish handed her a cell phone.

"I have sent you a contract using that phone."

There was silence as Trudie read it over. Finally, she looked up, bemusement across her face.

"You want me to eat blue cheese?"

Well, phew. Pranish dodged a lot of bullets from me with that one.

"Everyone here knows you wouldn't eat blue cheese. Not under any normal circumstances. But, by signing that contract with true intent, you will be compelled to do so."

"What if I can't garner up the true consent to do it?"

Pranish smirked, subtly. "Read the rest of the doc."

Trudie read a bit, mouthing the words, and then looked up, shocked. "If I do it, you'll give me your legendary hand-blaster in *Age of Aegis*? You love that gun. You'd never."

"I would. If you sign the contract and eat the blue cheese."

"How do I know you won't renege?"

"Lawmantic contracts are binding. Upon both of us signing, we will both be compelled to fulfil the contract within the timeframe specified. This one specifies ten minutes."

Trudie looked at the contract, consternation on her face.

"Blue fucking cheese," she mouthed.

"Fine," she said. "I'll do it."

"Excellent! Please press your finger to the button at the bottom of the contract. No need for signatures. The magic picks up on everything it needs to."

"I better get that fucking gun," Trudie said, placing her finger on the button.

Pranish displayed his screen to the crowd.

"I have received a notification that Trudie has accepted the contract. Now, I can either cancel it or accept it. I will be accepting it."

He pressed his finger to the screen.

I'd never seen someone who had signed a lawmantic contract before. I didn't know what to think about it.

Both Pranish and Trudie's faces didn't go blank, but they did focus. As if they had a single thing on their mind. Trudie sidled past the crowd, making a beeline to the snack table.

Pranish jogged to his room, where his computer was. Some followed him, others followed Trudie. I stayed put, leaning over my shoulder to the sound of shocked gasps as Trudie ate the food she hated the most in the world.

A guy exited Pranish's room. "He did it. He gave the blaster. And oh shit, I'd never do that in my life. That thing could one hit any boss lower than level 30."

"This stuff is fucking toxic," Trudie swore, running to the bathroom. I heard gagging and running water.

Pranish exited his room, looking simultaneously triumphant and dismayed. That hand-blaster was really something. He sure was making sacrifices.

Trudie exited the bathroom, still sticking out her tongue in disgust. She walked back to her spot next to Pranish.

"I got the email. Object transferred."

She looked stunned. And not just from the cheese.

The crowd looked on, not exactly sure what to make of it all. Pranish was about to speak, a new air of confidence coming over him, when there was a knock on the door.

Everyone looked at the door ominously, as if they all knew that nobody else was expected. A man looked through the eye-hole and turned to Pranish.

"It's your brother."

Well, that wasn't good. Arjun was a real prick. While Pranish was not the strongest of sorcerers, Arjun had enough spark to cause a blizzard. He probably would have given the Marshal a challenge. I didn't know who I'd want to win though. At least the Marshal was somewhat respectful.

Pranish made his way to the door, his every step reluctant, and opened it. Everyone stood. Even me. Trudie made her way over to stand next to me.

"You missed your spark therapy appointment," Arjun said, his voice as cold as his ice-powers. He walked into the room, causing Pranish to back away. The door swung closed behind him.

"I told you..." Pranish said, hushed, but we could all still hear. "I'm not wasting my time on that anymore."

"Wasting time? Is it a waste of time to get your powers up to a standard befitting your blood?"

Arjun looked up, only now realising that he had an audience.

"What's this?"

He noticed the PowerPoint.

"Talking of wasting time..." he snarled. "Wizardry. Pleb-work. Mom and dad have factories full of husks who need fucking words to cast. Imitators. And you want to be just like them – when we're meant for so much more."

"What? What are we meant for?" Pranish shouted, suddenly, clenching his fists. "Freezing lakes and killing all the fish? Slaughtering husks at the Three-Point Line? Lauding a mistake of birth over everyone around us? I don't want that, Arjun. I want to earn my power. With my brain. With grit."

Pranish held up his phone, the app still displayed.

"This is what I'm meant for. Not some fucking sorcery bullshit. That isn't going to change anything. This will."

Arjun glanced at the phone, and then it burst open, releasing a gust of icy wind. Some people cried out. Pranish just stared at his bloody hand, filled with ice and shrapnel form the cell phone.

"You're coming with me now, brother," Arjun said. "To tell mom and dad what you've just told me."

Trudie sidled up next to Andy and whispered to him.

"You gotta do something. This night means so much to him."

Andy didn't respond. I watched him, looking over towards Colin, who was standing off to the side.

"Oliver is moving to the door," Treth said.

I looked, and there he was. Standing there, looking menacing. He was also looking at Colin.

This wasn't good.

"No," Pranish said, lowering his hand. "I'm not going. This is my night, Arjun. And I've got guests."

Pranish turned but stopped. He looked down at his feet, which were now frozen to the floor. I winced. I knew the feeling of being trapped by ice too well.

"Andy, please go help him. Tell that asshole that your dad will do something. Threaten him. Anything. Please."

Andy ignored her completely and, as she touched his shoulder, he shoved her away and moved towards Colin.

This wasn't good at all.

Despite my limp, I started pushing through people, my hand drifting towards my knife. I wasn't planning on killing Andy. But…just in case.

"Let go of me, Arjun!" Pranish shouted, but there was a waver in his voice.

"Oliver and Andy are flanking him," Treth said. "Oliver is waiting by the door. No escape routes."

I had the nasty feeling that Andy was going to do something truly stupid. And I had to stop him.

"If you want to be let go, then use your powers," Arjun said. He backed away. "If you can. That is."

Pranish looked at him, staring daggers, and I knew that any last ounce of love Pranish might have had for his brother was now gone. But my focus was on something else.

I managed to catch up to Andy, who I grabbed by the shoulder.

"Don't…" I stopped. Andy's eyes were glowing yellow, like a predatory monster. I let go in shock, and he continued towards Colin.

"Colin," Andy said, his voice cold.

Colin looked at him, and smiled, that disarming smile.

"Hey. Good to see you. Think we can sort this guy out?"

Andy didn't reply.

"Oliver is moving," Treth said.

"Use your powers, Pranish! Show these people how much of a powerless loser you are."

"Um, Andy? What's up?" Colin said, looking a bit worried.

A person walked in front of me. I shoved them out of the way. My knife was drawn.

"Use your powers."

"You're standing a bit too close there, Andy…"

"Something is happening," Treth said, the sort of worry in his voice that he only had when something really bad was about to happen.

I shouted. "Colin!"

Just as Pranish shouted, "No!"

Oliver exploded into a red-mist, his upper torso and head catapulting across the room.

In that moment, Andy's body twisted, and Colin backed away, hitting the bookshelf behind him.

I beat people out of the way. Only a few more metres.

People screamed, and I heard gunshots. I didn't care.

Andy's arm grew in size, bulking up and roiling like it was possessed. His nails sharpened and extended, blackening, and his arm sprouted fur.

"Get down!" I shouted.

Colin reached for his waistband and drew out the gun I'd given him. He'd been carrying it. Even though he hated it.

A person tripped me up as they ran from something. I didn't know what. All that mattered was right before me.

"Fire!" I shouted.

Colin fired, and blood spurted from Andy's head. But he didn't collapse.

From the corner of my eye, I saw a pale figure wearing black sink their teeth into the neck of the girl I'd been arguing with. They didn't do it delicately, like in the movies. They ripped her head from her shoulders, letting blood spray.

I rushed forward, my knife drawn, when I was grabbed from behind. I sank my knife into the vampire's face, blinding it at least temporarily.

Colin fired again, and again. Andy grabbed him by his neck, and he dropped the gun.

"No!" I cried out. "Don't!"

It happened suddenly. A gush of blood. It stained Andy's hand, the skin and the sprouting fur. Colin's body collapsed, and I could only stare at it for a second before screaming.

"I'll kill you!" I screamed, tears escaping my eyes while all I felt was rage.

But when I tried to stand, my body felt numb. Andy fell to the floor. And so did the vampires. And Pranish. And Arjun, who held a vampire's head in an ice-cube.

Silence fell. And then the sound of unnatural footsteps. I knew what they were immediately. Undead.

The miasma was visible to me, yet I was awake.

Flesh puppets entered the room, pushed corpses out of the way, and then stood at attention by the door.

A young girl, wearing a black hoodie and jeans entered. She could not have been older than 14.

My breath caught in my throat and I couldn't breathe.

It couldn't be.

She looked around the room, saw me, and grinned.

She squatted by my head, blonde bangs covering a pair of hazel eyes. I couldn't speak but didn't know if I would even if I could.

She smiled, and her eyes lit up with excitement and derangement.

"A promise is a promise, Kitty Kat. Let's go home."

Afterword

Kat is a hard girl in many ways. She calls herself broken, but as her author, I don't believe that's the case. Kat may have been broken once, but as the archdemon in book 3 implied, she is broken no longer.

This book allowed Kat to become emotionally intimate. Out of all the books, I think this one has changed her views on humans and relationships more than any other.

Kat let herself love and be loved.

And keeping in mind what happened at the end, I think this may risk breaking her again.

But every reforging requires a breaking. And Kat will be reforged ever stronger. You can count on that.

Acknowledgements

While books are (often) the work of a single person, they take a veritable organisation to produce. I'm an independent author because I value my freedom and am sceptical of the traditional publishing industry. While this makes some aspects of my business easier, it also means that I lack a certain connection to an institution. Succinctly: this is a lonely career.

But there are people in my life who have helped me along and have been integral to the creation of this book and series.

It takes a lot of patience to write six books before releasing a single one, and without the feedback and conversation of my beta readers, Tyler Sudweeks and Chelsea Murphy, I would have gone insane a long time ago. Thank you!

I would also like to thank my mother for providing her editing skills to get these books into a condition fit for human consumption, and for being someone I can always natter to about Kat, Hope City and necromancy.

Thank you to Deranged Doctor Design for the wonderful cover art. I advise them to any author looking for a professional design.

And finally: thank you. Without you, this book would not be read and enjoyed. Without you, these words are just the scribblings of a half-mad author.

So, thank you!

And until next time.

Nicholas Woode-Smith is a full-time fantasy and science fiction author from Cape Town, South Africa. He has a degree in philosophy and economic history from the University of Cape Town. In his off-time, he plays PC strategy games, Magic: The Gathering, and Dungeons & Dragons.

Follow him on Facebook:

https://www.facebook.com/nickwoodesmith/

Made in the USA
Middletown, DE
27 March 2021